Take Me Home

Cameron Hart

Published by Cameron Hart, 2023.

Want a free book?

One look at the stunning waitress carrying the weight of the world on her shoulders, and I'm a goner. I wasn't looking for a sweet little thing with auburn hair and more baggage than I can fit on the back of my bike, but there's no going back now. She's mine. I'll prove to her I'm more than capable of handling her past and making her feel safe again.

---

1. https://dl.bookfunnel.com/7wbqvhsx8r

Connect with me!

Check out my website, cameronhart.net[2], for sneak previews on my latest projects.

Follow me on social media:

Facebook Page - facebook.com/cameronhartauthor
Instagram - instagram.com/cameron.hart.author
TikTok - tiktok.com/@author.cameron.hart
Goodreads - goodreads.com/16081533.Cameron_Hart
Bookbub - bookbub.com/authors/cameron-hart

---

2. https://cameronhart.net/

Chapter 1

Eli

It's official: I hate New York.

My flight was delayed, then canceled altogether. Apparently, not many people fly from Montana to NYC. Can't say I blame them. I have half a mind to tell this cab driver to turn around and take me back to the airport, but I need this job.

A hundred thousand dollars to be a bodyguard for a rich judge's daughter? I'd be a fool to turn down that kind of money, especially with the family ranch in dire straights.

I returned to my small hometown in the middle of nowhere Montana a few months ago to try and bring the old place out of the gutter. My father passed away three years ago, leaving everything to my mom. I didn't know how bad things were until I got a call from the bank about a second mortgage my mom took out for the ranch. Apparently, she's missed the last three payments and the ranch is about to go under.

Being the oldest son, I stepped up to the plate. I moved from Chicago, where a friend and I started our own security company, back home to Montana. At thirty-nine, it's not exactly what I had planned, but life has a way of happening when you least expect it.

A car horn blares on my right side, and the cab driver swerves to the left before jackknifing back into the right light. I grip the door handle and bite back a curse. *One hundred thousand dollars. One hundred thousand dollars,* I repeat to myself.

I found out about the job opportunity from my uncle, who is a high-power lawyer here in the city. He knew I used to run a security company out of Chicago. Judge Moretti just started a trial for a couple of guys with ties to the underground crime syndicate in New York and he's not leaving anything to chance with his family while the hearings take place.

I was supposed to be here hours earlier, but with my canceled flight and an extended layover once I found a new flight, I'm hours behind schedule. Instead of getting acclimated to my new space and setting up precautions for the judge's daughter, I'm in the back of a cab, staring at the meter ticking up, up, up. The damn thing soars to over fifty dollars by the time I get to the luxury apartments I'll be staying at with the Park Avenue Princess.

Annaya Moretti. According to my notes, she turned twenty-three on her last birthday. She's a party planner with a large group of friends, each one richer and more shallow than the last.

Sure, I've seen a picture of Annaya as well, and I must admit she's pretty.

Everything about her is...delicate. Her stunning blue eyes framed in long lashes pop against her olive skin and dark hair. I'm not sure how she ended up with blue eyes. They don't seem to match with her otherwise very Italian heritage and complexion. The combination is nothing short of magical.

Nope. Don't even start, I scold myself.

I shove that shit way down deep. It doesn't matter what she looks like. I'm simply observing that objectively, Annaya isn't hideous-looking. It's all part of the job to notice these things.

It may have been a while since I've done security work, but I know enough to do my homework before going on the job. The first rule is to be prepared for any situation. Surprises are not good when it comes to protecting others. So I researched the little princess I'd be babysitting these next few months.

She's my opposite in every way. Annaya comes from money, the kind that paid for an Ivy League education just so she can party plan. I chuckle to myself at what a ridiculous occupation it is. She probably puts on dinner parties for all of her posh, socialite friends. Who needs hundreds of thousands of dollars worth of education to plan a party? Sheesh.

Material things have never been important to me, but family is everything. Not so much with Ms. Moretti. Between the high-rise apartment, designer clothes, and hardly talking to her parents, I can safely say it's going to be a long-ass two months.

"It's worth it to save the ranch," I mutter to myself.

"What's that?" the cab driver asks.

"Nothin'," I grunt as I hand over a ridiculous amount of cash for the single worst car ride of my life.

After a shit day of travel and researching the brat I'll be stuck with, I'm in horrible mood. I suppose I better get used to it now, seeing as I don't think it'll be changing any time soon.

It's late, past midnight, and I want nothing more than to fall into a bed and sleep off this day. I haul my luggage up the elevator and get to the top floor. Annaya's father said she was out of town and would be on the first flight back to New York ASAP. He gave me the door code just in case I beat her back to her place, which it looks like I did.

I open the door and set my duffel bags and backpack on the floor. Walking to the kitchen – the modern, sleek, too fancy-to-actually-cook-in-here kitchen, might I add – I look in the fridge for something to drink.

As I'm elbow-deep sorting through organic Greek yogurt, fresh fruits, and some weird smoothie concoction that looks downright disgusting, I hear the beep of the code being entered. I assume it's the little princess herself, apparently having about as good of a travel day as me.

I close the fridge and head out to the entryway to introduce myself. Turning the corner, I see a petite brunette holding an iron fire poker like a baseball bat, stalking her way toward the kitchen.

My first thought is that she's gorgeous and the photos I looked at earlier do not do her justice. Even with a messy bun, no makeup, sweatpants, a t-shirt, and no doubt hours of travel weighing on her tiny shoulders, she's easily the most beautiful woman I've ever seen.

My second thought is that she's got some fight in her and I can't deny how sexy I find that.

Shit, man, get it together. She's a job, nothing more.

"Who the fuck are you and why are you in my apartment?" Annaya spits out at me.

Amazingly, there's no fear in her eyes. No, she's all feisty and fired up, despite me being a foot taller and a solid hundred pounds bigger than her.

"I'm your new bodyguard. Didn't your dad tell you?" I try to smile as I put my hands in front of me to show her I'm no threat.

"Bodyguard?" she asks incredulously. Annaya startles me by barking out a laugh, dropping the fire poker from its position over her shoulder.

I can't help but enjoy the sweet sound. It's been way too long since I've had any kind of joy in my life. I've been buried in bills and stress for the last six months. Even before then, though, when was the last time I was just...happy?

As if suddenly remembering I'm here, Annaya straightens up and points the fire poker right at me.

"That line might have worked with the other trust fund babies in this building, but I know my father wouldn't hire a bodyguard for me. You better tell me what you're doing in my apartment right the fuck now or else I'm calling the cops." She thrusts the fire poker in my direction to emphasize her point.

Alright, this is getting less cute and more annoying by the moment.

"Annaya, I am your bodyguard. Your father, Presley Moretti, gave me the code for your apartment. That's how I got in here and that's how I know your name."

"That doesn't mean a damn thing," she counters. "My dad is a high-profile judge so it's no surprise you know his name. I'm assuming you can google things like addresses and family members of judges. Plus, a ruggedly handsome guy like yourself probably sweet-talked the attendant downstairs to let you up. It wouldn't be the first time."

My mind keeps catching on *ruggedly handsome*. I can't help but swell up a little bit with pride that she finds me attractive. Not that it matters.

That last part, however, about this not being the first time someone made it up to her apartment, has my protective instinct setting in. I make a mental note to have the doorman fired. Come to think of it, he didn't even question me when I said I knew Annaya and her dad. It was one in the morning, why would anyone be visiting her? I was too tired to notice, and honestly, just grateful I didn't have to put up a fight. Speaking of...

I've already come up with three ways to disarm Annaya and restrain her from hurting me or herself, but I want her to trust me.

"Call your dad, then, if you don't believe me."

She stares at me for a second, assessing me. Then I see a faint blush stain her cheeks as she rolls her eyes and flares her nostrils like she's annoyed at herself for not thinking of that.

"Fine. I will." Annaya is trying to be tough and maintain control of the situation, but it's coming off more as a toddler having a temper tantrum. It's pretty fucking cute, even though I'm still annoyed. *What is it about this girl?*

She whips out her phone and calls her dad, putting him on speakerphone.

"Why are you calling me at this hour?" comes Presley's harsh voice.

"Presley, did you forget to tell me something?"

Why doesn't she call him dad? *Typical brat.*

"I don't have time for games. Tell me what you need to tell me and let me get back to bed."

What's his deal? The man is paying a pretty penny for me to protect his daughter, so obviously he thought she could be in some sort of danger. What if she called him because she felt threatened?

"A large man is standing in my apartment claiming to be my bodyguard that you hired."

He sighs like she's an annoying child. "Yes, Annaya. He's your bodyguard. I'm on a tricky case with some bad guys and I just want to make sure you are safe while they are on trial."

Her face twists in confusion and unbelief.

"But why..." she trails off.

"Look, is that all? I'd like to get back to sleep."

"Yeah," Annaya whispers before hanging up. She looks down at her feet and her shoulders slump just a little bit.

"Mind putting that down, princess?" I ask with a teasing smile, hoping to diffuse some of her tension.

Annaya growls at me and it's the hottest fucking sound I've ever heard. My dick twitches.

Down, boy.

"Don't you ever call me that," she says as she steps closer, lightly stabbing me in the stomach with the fire poker. "Fuck you."

She drops the fire poker on the floor in front of my feet. It makes a loud clanging as it hits the tile flooring in the kitchen. I watch as she turns on her heel and storms off to what I assume is her bedroom.

Damn, this woman has some fire. And a seriously terrible attitude. She may be sexy as fuck, but everything I've researched about her and now experienced first-hand tells me this is going to be a *very* long two months.

Chapter 2

Annaya

Walking into my apartment to find a strange man rummaging through my fridge was *not* the best end to an already shittastic day.

Part of me knows I was a bitch and should turn around and apologize to the man who was hired to protect me. The bigger part of me, however, is too damn tired to care. I swear I can feel his gaze follow me down the hall, and I can't say I don't like it. Too bad he saw me at my absolute worst.

Seven hours ago, I was in LA getting the last details arranged for the fundraiser I've been organizing for the last six months. As an event planner, it's my job to get the best of the best and to make sure everything is perfect, down to the last flower arrangement. And these flowers were going to be the crowning jewel.

While the fundraiser is here in New York, the flowers I have in mind are native to the California coast. I was about to get everything squared away on a deal for fresh flowers to be flown in the morning of the fundraiser when Presley called.

My father demanded I get on the next plane and come home. No explanation, just the marching order to be back in my apartment as soon as possible. I almost ignored him and confirmed my appointments for the next day.

However, there's some part of me that still longs for his approval, so I packed up and got on the next flight to New York. After rearranging my whole schedule to fly home, enduring three layovers, and fighting off a migraine, I was in no mood to deal with Mr. Tall-Muscled-And-Devilishly-Handsome standing in my kitchen.

I need a shower and about twelve hours of uninterrupted sleep. Unfortunately, just the shower will have to do. Now I'm way behind schedule, thanks to Presley, so I'll have to get an early start tomorrow.

As soon as I shut my bedroom door, I start stripping off my grungy plane-ride outfit, trailing clothes all the way to my en suite bathroom. Yes, a hot shower is exactly what the doctor ordered.

My tense muscles finally relax as the warm water hits my skin. I take my time washing up, running through my new, updated to-do list for the fundraiser now that my original plans have been somewhat de-railed.

Hours later, I wake up feeling hungover as hell, but I know it's just the jetlag. I roll over and look at the clock. seven am. Today is going to be a long-ass day.

I walk out to the kitchen and get coffee started before grabbing a Greek yogurt out of the fridge. I'm digging through the silverware drawer for my favorite mini spoon when I hear a bear growling in my living room.

"Why are you up so early?"

I jump, sending several spoons clattering to the floor.

"Shit!" I squeal. I forgot about...whatever his name is.

"And what the fuck are you wearing?"

Double shit.

I've never had a roommate, so I've never had to worry about walking around in my PJs. Or in this case, lack thereof. Just have on the tank top I wore to bed last night and my panties.

I'm a little embarrassed, but I can't let him see that. I don't want him to have any sort of upper hand on me. This man, who I've barely met, makes me feel vulnerable and on edge.

"Good morning to you too, grouchy pants."

"At least I'm wearing pants," he grumbles.

I fight the slight blush that threatens to creep up my cheeks.

"Do you want some coffee? We've got a busy day ahead of us. Can't have you holding me back because you're too tired."

He grunts and runs a hand through his adorably messy hair. I didn't get a good chance to look at him last night, I just saw that he was large and rippling with chiseled muscle. But now I see he has dark brown hair, a little on the long side, and hazel eyes that I could get lost in if I'm not careful.

There's no denying this man is gorgeous.

And he'll be living with me for how long?

He stands up from the couch and walks toward the kitchen.

In an attempt not to gawk at him in his low-slung sweatpants, I turn around and start a conversation.

"Why'd you sleep on the couch? There are two other bedrooms in my apartment. Or are you used to couch-surfing?" I know I'm being a brat. I don't understand the way he's making me feel, so I'm hoping to put some distance between us.

"I didn't know where you wanted me so I just stayed out here."

"I thought Presley would have told you where to sleep. He didn't mind giving you the code to my door. Though, in his defense, he's never been here. Maybe he didn't know."

"Did you just move in?"

"Nope. Been here for four years."

"And your dad hasn't come for a visit?"

I shake my head, regretting saying anything. The less we talk about my family, the better.

"That's a shame," he says, surprising the hell out of me. "It's a nice place you have here."

I look at him, not sure what to do with his comment. He has a sincere look in his eyes, intense and questioning. He's being nice. I don't like it.

"I don't need anyone's approval, least of all yours."

He gives me an exasperated look. I don't blame him. I'm being a bitch right now. I turn away from him and bend down to pick up the spoons I dropped earlier. Again, forgetting I'm just in some cotton panties until I hear a growl come from behind me.

I stand up and turn back toward my bodyguard. I don't miss the growing bulge in his sweatpants. A wicked thought creeps into my head, and try as I might to banish it, my body moves on its own.

He likes what he sees? This could be fun.

The large man takes a step back, leaning against the counter. I take a step toward him and he flares his nostrils. Then, I open the cupboard behind him and grab two mugs before turning around and walking to the coffee maker. My bodyguard just stands there clenching his fists. Opening the fridge to grab the creamer, I make a little show of bending over, well aware that my ass is in full view.

I turn around and set the creamer on the counter, gasping softly when I feel his presence and heat behind me. I have to bite back a moan when a large pair of hands grip my hips. He's caging me in against the counter and I hang on to the edge as I feel the hard muscles of his abs and chest press into my back.

"Are you trying to seduce me, Annaya?" I feel his breath tickle the back of my neck before he places a soft kiss there.

I forget to breathe for a second. His lips move in a slow trail down my shoulder.

"Seduce you?" I manage to breathe out. "I don't even know your name..."

I lose my train of thought when I feel his teeth lightly scraping up my neck, stopping to nibble that sensitive spot just below my ear. My core clenches and my breath catches in my throat. Dammit, my panties are wet.

The man has no idea what this simple touch is doing to me. He continues to trail his lips ever so slowly up and down my neck while I melt for him. He removes his hands from my hips and lightly ghosts his fingers up my torso, underneath my shirt. It's embarrassing how wet I am right now, but I can't seem to control myself.

I should be stopping this. Nothing can happen between us. I was just messing with him, but he totally called my bluff. The thing is, I'm pretty much ready to jump in bed with him right this second. Not that I would have any idea what to do once I got there, but still.

His fingers continue their slow path up my ribs, tickling and teasing my skin. The rough pads of his fingers send shivers down my spine. He reaches my breasts and barely grazes his thumbs on the sensitive underside. Then he stops, holding me by my ribcage in his big, capable hands.

I feel him drag my earlobe through his teeth and my back arches, pressing my ass back into him, sliding up and down his large, hard cock. His hands slide back down my body, over my tummy, and grip my hips once more, stilling my motions but pressing me further into his massive erection. I feel his lips graze the shell of my ear.

"I'm Eli," he says. The rumble of his voice vibrates through me, making another mess in my panties.

Then he lets me go, reaching around me to grab a mug before walking to the other counter where the coffee maker is.

Chapter 3

Eli

Shit.

I shouldn't have done that. She was teasing me, walking around in her underwear for Christ's sake, bending over, giving me a show. I wanted to put my hands on her the second I opened my eyes and saw her toned legs and tight ass. I restrained myself as long as I could.

I only meant to tease her back. I was going to stand behind her and hold her hips, and maybe, *maybe* kiss her neck if she didn't slap me in the face first.

But as soon as I touched her, I was gone. I needed to feel more of her skin, press her closer to me. I wanted to strip her clothes off and fuck her right there in the kitchen. I wanted to lick every inch of her pussy until she screamed my name.

Fuck.

I've never wanted anyone this bad, never experienced this pull before. This longing. This need. *I need to be inside of her.*

Annaya finally catches her breath and turns around, face flushed. I drag my eyes over her luscious, lithe body and notice her pebbled nipples as well as a wet spot on those adorable cotton panties she has on.

I grin at her as I adjust my throbbing cock, making no effort to hide what I'm doing. Her eyes immediately move to my crotch and my dick grows even harder at her attention.

"Eli..." she breathes out, and fuck if I don't like my name on her lips. "I...that...we shouldn't have done that."

I grin at her again. Her tone betrays her. I can tell she wants more, but I'll respect her wishes.

"Whatever you say, princess," I say with a wink.

And just like that, the spell is over. Her eyes become cold as steel as her fists tighten at her sides.

"I said not to call me that," she yells and stomps her foot.

Goddamn, the temper on this woman. I wouldn't mind letting her work out some of her frustration on my cock.

Stop it.

She's right. This can't happen. No matter how much I want her.

"I'm going to go get ready for the day. We have a busy schedule," Annaya says in a clipped tone. "I suggest you clean up too, I don't want you scaring off my clients. The guest bathroom is the second door on the left, next to my room."

With that, she storms out of the kitchen for the second time in twenty-four hours and heads to her room. I watch her leave, unable to keep my eyes off of her perfect, juicy ass. I remember how amazing it felt pressed up against my aching cock. And the taste of her skin, how she responded to my touch...

Shit.

I pick up my bags and wander down the hall to find the bathroom and rinse off.

With the hot water dripping off my back, my thoughts turn once again to Annaya. I shouldn't be indulging in the fantasy, but if I'm going to spend all day around her, I have to relieve this tension somehow.

I grab my still-hard cock at the base and stroke up and down, picturing Annaya on her knees in front of me. She looks up at me with those stunning blue eyes of hers and wraps her mouth around the monster between my legs.

I imagine her eyes fluttering closed, those long lashes fanning out over her delicate cheeks as she moans around my girth. I can almost feel the vibrations from her voice around my cock now. I grunt, possibly a little too loudly.

I continue to stroke, faster now. Rougher. I'm so lost in the fantasy, I swear I can hear her sexy little moans.

Wait.

I shut the water off and stand closer to the wall that shares her room.

"Mmmm, yeah..."

Oh, fuck.

Is she doing the same thing I am?

"Yes...!" she whimpers, unaware that she answered my question perfectly.

That's so fucking hot. Her sounds, the way she unabashedly chases her own pleasure, the fact that my touch had the same effect on her as hers did on me. I stroke myself harder, faster, wanting to match her intensity. I picture pinning her against the wall of the shower, her legs gripping my hips as I slam into her again and again.

I grunt and I hear her moan again through the wall.

I imagine Annaya throwing her head back and moaning as I rut into her and then lean down and suck her hard nipple.

"Ah, ah, ah..." Her sexy little sounds are getting higher, more desperate. I can tell she's close. Fuck, I can feel her walls starting to pulse around me as I draw out our pleasure. She shakes in my arms and I grip her ass tighter, pumping her body up and down my cock.

"Fuck, *ELI*!"

I lose it. Hearing my name as she shouts her climax does me in. I fucking shoot my cum all over the shower wall, rope after rope. I'm shaking as I reach out a hand on the wall to steady myself as my cum keeps spurting out of me.

When I finally come down from my release, I turn the water back on, washing away the evidence of my intense orgasm.

Twenty minutes later, I'm somewhat under control again. I've cleaned up and changed into what I hope is an acceptable outfit for her prissy clients, and now I'm sitting on the couch, waiting for her highness to come out of her room.

When she finally emerges, I have to catch myself from gawking at her. She's wearing a red dress that wraps around her body, secured by a tie at her hip, paired with some black stilettos. Her hair falls down her back in long, chocolatey waves. She doesn't have much makeup on, just enough to accent her already beautiful features.

The only thing I can think about is undoing the knot that holds her dress together and seeing what matching bra and panty set she's wearing because I know a woman like this has a matching set on.

I clear my throat. "You look nice," I say.

Yeah, by "nice" I mean, "Incredibly fucking sexy."

She looks at me strangely. Is that a blush spreading out over her cheeks? I wonder if she's thinking about this morning in the kitchen, or whatever fantasies she indulged in while pleasuring herself.

Annaya snaps out of it, straightening her back and narrowing her eyes at me. "Try to keep your hands to yourself, *Eli.*" She says my name like it's a swear word.

It seems as if we're back to her being a brat.

I stand up as she gathers all of her things in a huge over-the-shoulder bag. Cell phone, binder, calculator, pens, a sketch pad, and a laptop. I wonder if her tiny body can even lug all that stuff around, but she manages to slip it over her shoulder just fine.

Annaya turns toward the door and walks out without another word to me. I'll take that as my cue to follow her.

Outside, I slip into bodyguard mode. I can't afford to be distracted. I move behind her and sweep the perimeter with my eyes. There's a car waiting outside for us, of course. I'd expect nothing less for the little princess. The sexy princess. Dammit. It's going to be a long day. A long two months.

Chapter 4

"So, what's on the agenda today, boss?" Eli asks.

I roll my eyes at his new nickname for me, though it's better than princess. Anything is better than that.

"Right now we're going to a meeting with the fundraiser board. Who knows how long that will last."

"Fundraiser?"

"Oh crap," I mutter to myself. How am I going to explain a six-and-a-half-foot muscled Greek god following me around the black tie event?

"What is it? What's wrong?" Eli startles me with his intensity.

"I was just thinking about the fundraiser," I say once I clear my throat. Eli's shoulders relax and I see his grip loosening on his gun. I hadn't even noticed him reaching for it. Good to know he really does take my safety seriously. That shouldn't make me feel all warm and fuzzy inside, but it does. Dammit.

"Annaya?"

Why does my name have to sound so good coming from his lips?

"I was just thinking about how to explain your presence at the fundraiser."

Eli bristles. "Afraid I'll embarrass you?" he mutters.

"No. I was just trying to think of a way to make you more..." I trail off, sweeping my hand up and down his massive frame. "Subtle. I need you to be more subtle."

"I'll be your date," he says with an easy shrug.

I'm trying hard not to blush, but dang it, I feel my face heating. My mind flashes to this morning, the way his rough hands felt trailing over my skin, his lips tickling my ear, and his thick, heavy cock. Good *lord*. I'm ashamed to admit I touched myself while Eli was in the shower, but

I couldn't stop. My orgasm was quick and fierce, but still left me feeling empty and achy.

"Fine," I manage to say. My voice didn't even crack, so I consider that a win. I snap back into professional mode. It's not like it's a real date or Eli is my real boyfriend. "After the fundraiser board, I'm meeting with a vendor in Midtown, then having lunch with a potential client at twelve-thirty."

I'm busy answering emails on my phone while the car takes us to my first appointment. I realize Eli hasn't said anything in a few minutes, so I pause and look over at him. He has a weird look on his face like I spoke in some foreign language.

"What?" I snip. "Were you expecting to just sit around my apartment and watch Netflix all day while I lounged by the pool and sipped martinis? Hate to break it to you, but I'm a busy woman. I'll need you to keep up with me or else I can have the driver drop you back off at my apartment."

His look changes from confused to pissed off. Good. I can handle pissed off.

"Calm down, woman. I was just thinking that you have a very full schedule for someone who was supposed to be out of town for the next few days."

"Oh."

"*Oh?* That's all you have to say after your little outburst?"

"Outburst?" Oh, this man. "*Outburst?* Look, you were hired by Presley to do a job, even though I don't think your presence is necessary in any way whatsoever. I'm working on a huge project right now and the last thing I need is an unwanted complication. Which is exactly what you are."

I glare at him to emphasize my point. The bastard doesn't even blink.

"And not that it's any of your business," I continue, "but I had my appointments moved around as soon as I knew I'd be back in town early. I don't have the luxury of a day off with this fundraiser so close. Everything has to be perfect."

"Oh, darlin' that's where you're wrong. It is absolutely my business. I'll need a copy of your schedule. Do you have an assistant or something who can email me your calendar?"

Is he serious right now? "No."

"No, you don't have an assistant, or no, you won't have them email me your calendar?" Eli asks in a slow and controlled voice like I'm a stupid kid who needs the instructions repeated five times in a row.

"Both. Not that you care, but I'm in the first year of starting my event planning business and I don't have any full-time employees yet. So, no assistant. And also, no, I won't email you my calendar."

"Annaya..." he growls.

"You can stay at my apartment, eat my food, drink my booze, and follow me around while I work. Who knows, maybe you'll make a good assistant?" I quip. He doesn't get to know everything about me. I have things I want to keep private.

"I *will* get your schedule one way or another, but I suppose that's neither here nor there. Let's get one thing straight," he says, his voice deep and gritty. "Where you go, I go. That means *everywhere*. Work, restaurants, home, shopping, the salon, or whatever other shit you girls do. I'm there. That's what I'm paid for."

I can tell I'm not going to get anywhere with him right now, so I opt for the silent treatment until we get to my first appointment.

***

The rest of the day passes by without incident. Well, except for when Eli asked why I wanted to be a party planner as if *event* planning and *party* planning are even remotely the same things. The way he said it was so infuriating like I'm just some bimbo who wants an excuse to spend money on cocktails and evening gowns.

He pretty much stayed silent after that and kept himself scarce during my meetings. Every once in a while, I'd sneak a glance at him in his black, button-down shirt with the sleeves rolled up, his forearms showing off corded muscle and the hint of a tattoo peeking out. He was always staring right back at me, but I'm trying not to make too much of it. It's his job to look out for me, so of course he's keeping his eyes on me.

Not that it matters anyway.

We're finally on the way back home now. It's almost seven-thirty and I'm completely wiped. I close my eyes and lean my head back on the headrest.

"You look tired," Eli says, echoing my thoughts.

"I feel tired," I retort, not opening my eyes.

He chuckles softly and I'd be lying if I said that sound didn't warm me up inside. Not just in a sexual way, but in a comforting way. I can't help the smile that pulls on the corner of my lips.

"Are your days always this long?"

"They have been lately. It's just this fundraiser. It's really important to me and I want to do well. My parents are going to come to this one. They haven't been to anything I've planned yet, but I know this one means something to them too. Or at least I hope it does." *Oh, god, what am I even saying?* "I... I'm sorry, I don't know why I told you all of that."

Flustered, I fiddle around with something in my purse. *What is Eli doing to me?*

"It's for cancer research, right?" he asks, mercifully ignoring my word vomit.

I nod. "Leukemia."

He waits for me to elaborate, but I don't.

"Any particular reason why it's so important to your family?"

Nope. Can't go there. Not with him.

"What do you want for dinner?" I ask, changing the subject. "We can order whatever. Do you like Chinese? There's a great place that delivers."

He furrows his brow and looks like he's going to say something, but then shakes his head. Eventually he sighs.

"Yeah, who doesn't like Chinese food?"

Chapter 5

Eli

We step inside and Annaya immediately kicks her heels off, which takes a good four inches off of her height. I'm worn out from walking around all day and I had on sturdy boots. Her feet must be killing her. I'm honestly pretty impressed.

A lot about Annaya is impressive, though. I didn't realize she was an *event* planner, which is different from a *party* planner, as I found out when I had the nerve to ask her why she got into her chosen profession.

God, the woman is so infuriating.

And yet... there's something to her feisty temper that gets me all worked up.

Shit. Don't go there. Don't think about what her skin felt like or the citrus scent of her hair.

"I'm taking a shower," she says over her shoulder, already half-way down the hall.

Well, that's certainly not helping me keep my mind off of the curve of her hips or her perfectly small, perky breasts. God, I want to see the water drip from her olive skin...

"Eli?" she asks, startling me from my inappropriate thoughts.

I grunt something at her, unable to form a coherent thought at the moment. The little brat giggles, which both infuriates me and turns me the fuck on. Jesus, I'm in trouble.

After Annaya takes a shower and puts on some leggings and an old college sweatshirt, Harvard, of course, she takes out her phone and calls the Chinese restaurant.

"Hi, I'd like an order of beef broccoli, sweet and sour chicken, sesame chicken, pork fried rice, chicken lo mein, and egg rolls. Oh, and crab Rangoon. And an order of pot stickers. That's it."

I have to chuckle at the insane amount of food she just ordered. Who knew she could pack away take-out like a champ?

"Are you planning on having eight of your closest friends over for dinner?" I say with an amused grin once she hangs up.

She glares at me, but I can tell she's fighting a smirk. Her sapphire eyes shine mischievously, and god... *she's beautiful. Ethereal.*

"No, cowboy, it's just you and me," Annaya says. "I, for one, am starving. Plus I didn't know what you liked, and I'm guessing you have to eat like five thousand calories a day to keep up those muscles, right?"

Her eyes glide down my chest before she stops herself and turns her head. I smile knowing she likes what she sees.

"And," she adds, "Chinese take-out makes the best leftovers. Everybody knows that."

The enchanting woman walks to the couch, dragging her gigantic bag with her. Once seated, she pulls out her laptop and sketchbook, getting to work on more things for the fundraiser, I assume.

I take my cue to leave her be and go rinse off myself before the food gets here.

Twenty minutes later, there is an absolute feast set out on her coffee table.

"Well... dig in!" Annaya says before excitedly reaching for one of the containers and diving her chopsticks inside.

"So, at the risk of another argument..." I start. She looks up and quirks an eyebrow at me. "What got you interested in *event* planning?"

I think she might toss the piece of broccoli between her chopsticks right at me, but instead, she gives me a shy smile. I was not expecting it, and I kind of like it. A lot. *Too much.*

"Well, I always wanted to own my own business and be independent from my parents. I had a double major in business management and finance." I was not expecting that. "I guess I've always liked having a plan. It helped when...well, it just helps. It helped me. And I guess I'm pretty good at problem-solving. Combine that with charity work and a business degree, and things just sort of fell into place."

I wonder what she went through that she felt like she needed a plan. Not that it matters. I'm just being friendly, not getting her life story.

"It seems like you do very well for yourself. Your parents must be proud of you," I offer.

She looks down at her chopsticks and her shoulders fall a little, the same as when she talked to her dad on the phone. Again, I wonder what she's not telling me. And *again*, I remind myself I'm not here for her life story.

I change the subject and we chat for a while as we finish off what we can of the food.

After we're done, I stand up to collect the impressive amount of empty containers. Annaya gets up to help.

"We did good, huh?" I say, nodding toward the table. She laughs a little and the sound does something to me, just like it did the first time I heard it. It makes me feel... comfortable? I don't know. "Who knew the princess could pack it away?"

As soon as the words are out of my mouth, I know I fucked up. Her eyes turn icy and her muscles tense as she turns on her heel and stomps toward me.

Her smiles and laughter are cute, but her anger is sexy as fuck.

"What did I tell you about calling me princess, huh?" She's standing a foot away from me and I can feel the rage rippling off her.

I put my hands up in front of me in a sign of surrender and take a step back. She takes a step forward.

"I said not to call me that! Not ever!" She pounds her tiny fists on my chest, and I absorb her blows like they are nothing at all.

I'm not sure why she's so upset about this, but I really didn't mean to set her off. I just forgot. I guess I won't forget ever again.

She raises her right hand to slap me in the face, but I grab her wrist before she hits me. She tries with her other hand, and I grab that one, too. I pin her wrists at her sides. She's inches away from me, breathing heavily due to the physical exertion. I look in her eyes and see fierceness, anger... and hurt. Tears are burning behind her eyes and it fucking breaks something in me.

They aren't manipulative tears, they're raw emotion.

Right as the first tear falls, she crashes her lips into mine and my world fucking explodes. I don't miss a beat, opening up for her and letting her take control. *For now.*

Annaya wrestles with my tongue and clashes her teeth with mine in a frantic, passionate kiss. It's like nothing I've ever experienced; all-consuming, overwhelming all of my senses as I drown in her. She bites my lower lip and I growl into her mouth, dropping her wrists from my grasp and squeezing her ass instead.

I pull her into me, grinding her hot pussy against my growing cock. She moans at the contact and I take the opportunity to attach my lips to her neck, nibbling and licking right below her ear before slowly moving to the crook of her neck.

This shouldn't be happening. Maybe that's why it's so fucking hot.

Annaya wraps her arms around me and digs her fingernails into the skin at the back of my neck, pushing me further into her. I take the hint and start sucking on her shoulder, moving her oversized sweatshirt to expose more skin.

"Off," she moans. At first, I think she's telling me to get off of her, but then I realize she's tugging my shirt up. I quickly get rid of the offending garment, all too happy to be that much closer to her. "Now me," she says while lifting her arms.

I grab the hem of her sweatshirt and throw it off her body, revealing her bare breasts to me. They are perfect, just like I thought.

She dives back in and kisses me with such force, my breath is practically knocked out of my lungs. I knew she'd be fucking incredible. Everything she does turns me on. Usually, I like to be in control, but I have to admit, her taking charge is really doing it for me right now. I mean, *really* doing it for me. I'm harder than I've ever been, and we've only just kissed.

Annaya breaks the kiss and trails her lips down my neck, stopping to trace the tattoos on my chest with her tongue. It sends shivers down my spine and I almost blow my load before we even really start. Then she bites my nipple and I growl, bucking my hips. *Fuck* it feels amazing.

She shoves my sweatpants and boxers down to the floor and I kick them off. I hear her gasp at my throbbing cock and then I feel her hand wrap around it. She tugs. *Hard.*

"Shit! Annaya, I'm not going to last if you keep it up."

She grins at me. The little devil knows exactly what she's doing.

Annaya slides her leggings and panties down and stands before me gloriously naked. She has toned legs that lead straight to her wet pussy, dripping down the inside of her thighs. Her tiny, soft tummy looks so smooth, and her generous hips call for me to grip them and dig my fingers in. Her tits are flawless. Brown nipples top the little mounds that I can't wait to suck into my mouth. My gaze travels up her slender neck and over the delicate features of her face. When I get to her eyes, I see fire and determination. Fuck. She's fucking perfect.

Annaya pushes me back onto the couch and I'm all too eager to obey. She climbs up my lap, straddling me and kissing me fiercely. My hands slide up her thighs and grip her hips. She claws down my chest and I fucking roar into her mouth. I love everything she does, every way she touches me, bringing pain, leaving pleasure.

I feel her sitting up on her knees and covering the tip of my cock with her pussy.

Fuck.

"Baby, I don't have a condom."

"It's okay. I'm clean," she says between ragged breaths. "I'm on the pill. Please, Eli. I need this."

I look up at her and still see fire in her eyes, but I also see pain, like right before we kissed. If she wants to use me to fuck away her pain, I'll gladly let her.

"I'm clean too. Now, ride me, Annaya."

She impales herself on my cock and we both cry out.

She's so goddamn tight, I'd swear she's... "Are you a virgin?" I grunt, every muscle in my body tensing to the point of pain.

"Not anymore," she rasps against my ear.

A hundred thoughts slam into my mind at her confession. Confusion as to why she didn't say anything, why she chose me, why now? Guilt tugs at my conscious as I stare into Annaya's eyes. She deserves better than a hard fuck on a couch for her first time, but at the same time, she needs this. I feel it. Feel her restless energy, her desperate need to control something, someone. Maybe my little minx really needs someone to control *her* and make her feel safe.

Above all else, however, her whispered words make me feel possessive. She's fucking *mine*.

"Jesus," I groan, holding her trembling body still as she slowly relaxes and opens up for me. "That's it, baby. Nice and slow. I'm gonna make you feel so good."

She moans, nodding her head as she wiggles her hips. I love feeling every inch of her pussy, memorizing her from the inside out. Her heat surrounds me and squeezes my cock. She takes me deeper, grinding her hips into me.

Annaya weaves her fingers in my hair and rips my head back, diving in for another wild kiss as she bounces on top of me. I reach between us and find her clit, rubbing frantic circles around the tight ball of nerves. I'm about to come and I need her to get there with me.

"Ah! Eli! *Fuuuuuck...*"

Annaya throws her head back and thrusts her tits in my face. I immediately start licking her nipple and then suck her breast into my mouth, earning me another sexy moan. I kiss and nibble my way over to her other breast, stopping to lick a path between them.

She tastes incredible, sweet and spicy, and something that's just her. I want to lick every inch of her body and make her come on my tongue.

I feel my orgasm building and I continue to stroke her clit and suck her gorgeous tits. Her legs start shaking and I know she's close.

"Come for me, Annaya," I say into her chest. She moans and her muscles tense. I can tell she's holding on, ever the stubborn woman.

I pinch her clit and bite down on her nipple. *Hard.* Her body goes completely still on top of me.

And then she screams as her orgasm overtakes her body. Her pussy clamps down on my hard cock again and again, so tight it almost hurts. Her thighs clench around my hips and she digs her nails into my shoulders, leaving her mark on every part of me. I've never seen anyone come so hard. She's stunning, beautifully shattered by her pleasure.

Her pussy is still pulsing around me and I continue to circle her clit again with my thumb.

"Oh, fuck, oh, fuck, fuck," she chants.

The goddess jerks her hips, rubbing me just right, and I pull another orgasm from her right as I shoot my load. Rope after rope pours into her and she takes it all. I grab her hips and move her up and down my shaft, still coming in powerful sprays.

"Jesus, fuck, so good baby."

We're both shaking and sweating. She rests her head on my shoulder and I reach up and stroke Annaya's back. A strange feeling comes over me, one that shocks me as much as settles me. I want to cuddle. I want nothing more than to wrap Annaya up in my arms and hold her, but I'm not sure what the protocol is here.

She opens her eyes, finally recovering from her orgasm, and looks at me. I see overwhelming vulnerability in her eyes, so many emotions floating just beneath the surface. There's more to Annaya than the stuck-up brat she was all day today.

But then something changes, it's like I can see her walls coming back up. Her brow furrows and she straightens up in my lap, slipping me out of her. I watch as she stands up and collects her clothes, holding them in front of her body like she's now embarrassed.

"I... we... we shouldn't have done that. I shouldn't have done that. I'm sorry, Eli. It won't happen again."

And with that, she turns and runs toward her bedroom. I want to run after her, but I'm currently stuck on this couch. My bones are jelly. My mind is mush. This woman just fucked me senseless and then told me it wouldn't happen again.

We'll see about that.

Chapter 6

Annaya

What the fuck did I just do?

I mean, I know I just had sex. Mind-blowing, life-altering sex. And, to top it all off, it was my first time. I can't believe I just... just threw myself at my bodyguard. I've never been like that, so demanding and in control. Something about Eli makes me crazy, and I can't decide if it's a good crazy or a bad crazy.

I'm not even sure what the hell happened. I was pissed at him, which made me want to punish him. Tease him. Torture him. Somewhere along the way, Eli made me feel sexy, confident, and... wanted.

That's the scary part. I don't know how to do any of this. I've been content to be on my own. Mostly.

It gets lonely, sure, but I'm happy. Kind of.

Even if I'm not happy, starting something with my bodyguard isn't going to help. Eventually, he'll leave me, once I've served my purpose. I'm never enough on my own, I have to be the supporting role. That's quite literally the reason I was born.

Not to mention that he's being paid to protect me. I basically forced myself on him and now he's trapped here.

Fuck.

Why am I so messed up? What the hell came over me?

I head to the shower to rinse off the sex and sweat still lingering on my skin. No matter how much I scrub, I can't wash away the feeling of his lips on mine, his teeth on my skin, his fingers on my clit, his huge cock stretching my pussy.

I'm so screwed.

***

The next morning, I'm awake before my alarm goes off. I've barely slept, but I still have a lot to do today, so the show must go on, as they say.

Walking into the kitchen, I see Eli ready to go, looking as sexy as ever. The man can really wear a pair of jeans. He's got two mugs out for coffee, which is already brewed in the pot.

He smiles at me, tentatively. I can tell he's going to let me take the lead on this one, which I'm grateful for.

I walk over and grab a mug, filling it up with coffee. *Yeah, I'm going to need a lot more than this to get through my day.*

"About last night," I start, my eyes looking down in my coffee mug, unable to meet his. "I'm sorry. It was my mistake. I shouldn't have taken advantage of you. I know this is your job, and I just...I don't know what came over me."

I clear my throat, trying to put on my best professional voice. I set down my coffee mug, straighten my shoulders and look him in the eye.

"So. I'm sorry. It won't happen again. Strictly professional from here on out," I try again.

I stick my hand out for a handshake because apparently, I'm a dork and clearly have no idea what else to do.

He takes my hand, but instead of shaking it, he pulls me toward him so we're chest to chest. I crane my neck up to look at him. His arms wrap around my waist, pulling me even closer. My hands automatically go to his large chest. Eli leans down, and I think he's going to kiss me, but instead, he ghosts his lips up my neck and tugs my earlobe between his teeth.

God, it feels so good.

"Baby, you can take advantage of me any time. I can't wait to do it again. But I won't make a move until you ask."

I'm practically panting, and I'm for sure going to have to change my panties before leaving the apartment.

Eli pulls back a little bit and places the most delicate kiss on my forehead. It's so different from what our dynamic has been, and I can't say I don't melt a little bit at his sweet gesture.

But then I remember my resolve to keep him at arm's length. I push him back and stumble into the counter, catching my hip on the corner.

I hiss out a breath and Eli reaches out to steady me, concern flashing in his eyes.

I swat his hand away. "I'm fine. Please don't touch me again, Eli."

My body screams in protest, already imagining his hands roaming over my body, but my mind is made up. I'm no good for him and I refuse to let him in any further.

He steps back and puts his hands in his pockets.

"Right," he says before clearing his throat. "What's on the agenda today, boss?"

His tone is cold. Detached. Just like I want it.

Why then does it hurt to hear his clipped voice?

I clear my head of those thoughts and focus on Eli's question. My agenda. Now that I can handle.

"I'm checking out the venue for the fundraiser at nine thirty, running over the last-minute details with a member of the board, stopping by the bank, late lunch with a client, and then I have a personal appointment in the afternoon, which you will not be attending."

"The fuck I'm not. I thought we went over this. I go wherever you go."

"Not for this. I'll be fine. The driver will be there."

"Good. So will I."

I feel my anger bubbling to the surface. "We will discuss this later," I snip. "You're going to make me late to my first meeting."

"We can discuss it all you want but my answer will be the same."

I roll my eyes and start to gather my things for the day. I walk out of the apartment without another word, going so far as to slam the door in his face as he follows me out.

Chapter 7

Eli

I roll my eyes at the dramatic Park Avenue princess and open the door to her apartment, following her out. Annaya doesn't even acknowledge me as I jog to catch up to her, sliding into the elevator right before the doors close.

She's maddening. Annaya is stubborn, rude, and a myriad of other adjectives that make my blood boil.

She's also confident, decisive, stunning, and delicious. I don't know what it is about her that's gotten so far under my skin. Well, aside from the mind-blowing sex last night. And god, she was a virgin. I should feel like an asshole, but instead I feel... possessive. But it's more than just sex.

Maybe it's her graceful movements, even in those ridiculous heels. Or how she furrows her brow and nibbles on the corner of her lip when she's concentrating. Maybe it's the way she smiles with her clients and vendors, building a good rapport and going the extra mile.

I wish she'd smile and laugh with me.

Dammit. I'm already so fucked. I know she's pushing me away, and I should let her. I really should. I really, *really* should.

But deep down I know I won't. I know I'll chase her. I love the challenge, love her fight. Love her moans of pleasure, love her brilliant eyes. Love...

Nope. *Shit.* It's been two days.

Annaya is right. Strictly professional. I can do that. It's only a few months. Then I'll be back home in Montana and this whole trip to New York will be all but forgotten.

Even as I think the words, a pit opens up in my stomach.

I won't forget Annaya. How could I? And as for the leaving her here in New York part? Yeah, I don't fucking like that idea either.

The elevator doors ding open, startling me from my thoughts. Annaya's six-inch heels click on the marble floor of the lobby as she makes her way out to her chauffeur. Yet another stark reminder of how incompatible we are. We grew up in two opposite worlds and value completely different things.

I'll have to keep reminding myself of that every time my treacherous heart decides to beat a little faster for her.

The rest of the day goes by pretty smoothly. Annaya is busy beyond belief. I think she's scheduled damn near every minute of her day. It's honestly fascinating to watch, though I'd never admit that to her.

We're getting in the car now, heading to her last stop for the day. I know she's going to fight me. In fact, I'm looking forward to it.

"Henry," Annaya addresses the driver. "You can take Eli home before our next appointment."

"I'm coming with you."

"The hell you are. I know you're here to watch over me or whatever, but this is personal. You can't be there. I deserve some privacy."

"I wasn't hired to protect you on your terms. I was hired to protect you on your father's terms, and he says I shadow you all the time. Those are my marching orders, and that's what I'm going to do."

"If you don't want to be dropped off at the apartment then you can get out here and walk. Your choice."

It's cute that she thinks she's going to get rid of me.

I don't say a word. I don't make a move. I simply absorb the deadly glares she's giving me, not reacting at all.

Henry, good man that he is, starts driving in the opposite direction of the apartment, toward what I'm assuming is the next appointment.

"Henry! Stop this car right now."

He puts the partition up, which makes me chuckle.

Annaya turns her attention back to me. "*Fuck you, Eli,*" she seethes, her tone low and malicious. She folds her arms across her chest and stares out the window.

I have no idea where we're going, but I can't say I'm not curious. Is she getting her hair done? Meeting friends? Meeting up with a boyfriend? That thought makes me tense up as anger boils in my blood.

I look over at Annaya, trying to gauge her emotions and maybe get a hint of what I can expect when we get to our destination.

She looks absolutely miserable and lost. Her brow is knit together and her eyes are closed as she leans her forehead against the window.

Upon further inspection, I notice her arms aren't crossing over her chest in anger. They seem to be hugging her waist, like she's trying to literally hold herself together.

Where the fuck are we going?

I want to rub the tension away from her shoulders and smooth her hair out of her face. I get the sudden urge to kiss her temple and tell her she's going to be okay. These are foreign feelings for me, but the need to act on them makes my chest ache.

Eventually, the car pulls into a large cemetery.

Oh shit.

Annaya shoots a glare at me. "Are you happy now?"

I have no idea what to say to that. Of course, I'm not happy. I hate that she's had to experience loss in her life. In fact, this whole thing is affecting me more than it should, and I don't know what to do about it.

Annaya sighs heavily, finally turning to look me in the eye. "Stay here." She says it more like a question rather than a demand, letting me know not to mess with her. She's fragile right now, and I get the sense Annaya is not a woman who enjoys being vulnerable. "I'll be right over there." She points to a large headstone about thirty feet away.

I nod and she slips out of the car, taking her huge bag with her.

I watch her walk up to the grave and dig in her purse. She takes off her shoes and sits at the foot of the grave, tucking her legs underneath her and sitting on her heels.

Annaya has a book in her hands, and I watch as she opens it and begins reading. She looks so goddamn vulnerable. And beautiful. I wonder who she's visiting? A friend? A relative? What is she reading to them? How long ago did they die?

I know I'll never get the answers to these questions, but I feel like I need them. Need them like I need my next breath of air. Need to find the source of her pain and make it better.

After about twenty minutes, she closes the book and puts it away in her purse. Annaya sits there in front of the grave, tracing something on it.

Finally, she stands up and brushes the dirt off her clothes, making her way back to the car. She opens the door and slips inside. I see her eyes are red, no doubt from crying. It guts me, just like it did last night when I saw tears in her eyes.

She doesn't look at me, just stares out the window as we drive away. The more I learn about her, the more I want to peel back her layers and see all of her. I want her to tell me her secrets as well as her desires. I want all of her laid before me so I can protect her tender heart.

This is killing me. Being here with Annaya but not *being* with her like I want might actually be the death of me.

"It's her birthday today." It's barely a whisper.

My heart breaks for Annaya. I feel so helpless. I want to ask who she visited, but I have a feeling that's not the right thing to say.

"I'm so sorry, Annaya." It's stupid, inadequate, and cliché, but it's all I have at my disposal at the moment.

Nodding, she pulls her knees up to her chest before wrapping her arms around them. She stares out the window while I stare at her. My beautifully broken Annaya.

Chapter 8

Annaya

Eli has been my bodyguard for almost three weeks now. We've gotten into a routine of sorts, with no incidents like the first couple of days. We haven't touched and I haven't been a fool and cried in front of him.

Work has been a good distraction. I've been busier than ever with the fundraiser just two days away. My parents said they were coming, and I really hope they do. I got Elaine's favorite flowers and stocked the bar with Presley's favorite bourbon.

I've been pulling twelve-hour days for the last four days and I know Eli is tired. Hell, I'm tired too, but I also love this stuff. It's my passion. I can't imagine how bored he is just following me around everywhere, but I assume he's getting paid well.

We just got home after another long day. I immediately take my stupid shoes off and collapse on the couch. Eli goes into the kitchen and comes back a few minutes later with a glass of wine.

"Here, you deserve this."

"Oh, um, thanks," I say softly, confused at his nice gesture. I take a huge swig of wine and let it trickle into my system, melting my tense muscles just a little bit.

Eli lifts my legs up and sits on the other end of the couch, resting my feet in his lap. He's respected the whole "not touching me" rule, even though deep down I really want his touch. I dream of him doing filthy things to me.

He takes one foot in his hands and begins massaging it. I'm about to pull my foot away, but it feels *amazing*. His thumbs rub the arch of my foot, kneading small circles down to my heel. Eli holds the top of my foot with one hand and the heel of my foot with the other and begins gently rotating my foot, loosening up the stiff joints in my ankle.

"Oh God, Eli. That feels so good."

I tilt my head down and look at him. The smile he flashes me makes my stomach flip and my chest grow tight. He's so handsome, almost boyish when he smiles. "You deserve it. You've been running yourself ragged. In six-inch heels no less."

I chuckle. "Yeah, you gotta look the part for these people to take you seriously. I don't really care about the designer clothes and ankle-breaking shoes. But, I love what I do and this is the uniform."

I don't know why I told him all of that. I take another sip of wine, hoping to stop my word vomit.

"I think you look good in whatever you wear." He grins at me and I can't stop the blush that creeps up into my cheeks.

Is he flirting with me? I don't know how to do that. He switches feet and I moan when he starts massaging the heel of my right foot.

I swear I hear a growl from Eli.

"Baby, you're making it really hard to keep my promise."

"Well, I'd say you're already breaking it by giving me a massage."

What am I doing? I should shut this down.

He chuckles. "This is still part of my job. I'm supposed to protect you, right? Keep you safe? I need to make sure you didn't hurt your feet while they were trapped in those ridiculous shoes."

I smile and let him continue his massage, my body melting at his touch.

Eli's phone rings and he hops off the couch. "I'll be right back," he says before walking out the door.

Two minutes later he returns with pizza and breadsticks.

"Where did this come from?"

"I ordered it when we got home. They just delivered it."

I'm stunned. He's being so thoughtful, and I don't know what to do with that. Just, like, in general, let alone with him. I've been alone for so long, I'm not sure how to handle these kinds of nice gestures.

"Thank you, Eli. That's really... um, that's really nice of you. You didn't have to do that."

He just smiles and grabs some plates for us. We eat in silence for a while before Eli speaks up.

"How much longer will work be like this for you?"

"The fundraiser is the day after tomorrow, so just two more days. Then I'll pass out for a week." I grin at him, but to my surprise, he looks worried.

"I can tell you're exhausted. Is there any way you can take it easy tomorrow? You're pushing yourself too hard."

It's too much.

Too much concern. Too much attention. No one cares about me, not like this, and it feels too personal. I snap.

"Look. I appreciate this tonight," I gesture toward the pizza and wine. "But I don't need you taking care of me or going above and beyond your job description, okay? I've been doing just fine on my own for a long time now."

Eli never breaks eye contact with me. It's intense but I can't look away.

"I know you're strong and independent and you can take care of yourself. But that doesn't mean you have to be alone. It's okay to have help sometimes."

He's so sincere, his hazel eyes peering into the depths of my soul and rearranging something deep inside.

I break eye contact and stand up off the couch. I clear my throat, trying to regain control of the situation.

"Well...Thank you. I'm exhausted, I'm going to go to bed now."

I turn and practically run toward my bedroom, though every step away from him hurts for some inexplicable reason.

Chapter 8

Something shifted in Annaya last night.

She let her defenses down for a second and things were almost easy between us. Between the sexual tension, her temper, and my general assholeishness, the last few weeks have been a strain. But last night was different. Intimate. And it scared her.

I wanted to do something nice for her. She's been stressed and burning the candle at both ends. I thought maybe her mother would come over to visit at some point and the two of them could relax, but so far, it seems as though Annaya and her parents don't talk very often, if at all.

I talk to Presley every night to report that there have been no threats and that's about it. He never asks about her or volunteers information about her. It's all business.

I wonder what their relationship is like. Annaya seems anxious and also happy about her mom and dad coming to the fundraiser. Part of me wonders if she's working extra hard to impress them. Something about that makes my heart ache.

It's the day before the fundraiser and Annaya is running around all over the city like a chicken with her head cut off. We're in the fourth store, or *boutique* as Annaya so helpfully corrected me earlier.

The phrase, "bull in a china shop" comes to mind as I try to stay out of her way and station myself near the door. Her phone rings and she pulls it out of the oversized duffle bag she claims is a purse.

Her face drains of color and the hairs on my neck stand on end. She flickers her eyes over to me, narrowing them in annoyance, of course, and then hurries away to some other corner of the store. Sorry. *Boutique.*

A few minutes pass and she comes charging toward me, the items she previously had in her arms abandoned on the floor.

"What's wrong?" I ask.

"I – I need to get to Elaine."

Her frantic tone has all of my alarm bells going off.

"Elaine?"

"My mom. I need to get to her *now.*" She's snapping at me and almost yelling. I can tell it's because she's desperate, not because she's actually mad at me.

"Is she hurt? What's wrong?"

"She's fine, mostly, I just need to go." The look in her eyes tells me she doesn't have much fight left in her before she breaks down.

"Okay, I'll call the driver and we'll head over there."

"No," she grits out, rather forcefully. "You're not coming with me."

Not this shit again.

"Yes, I am. It's my job, remember?"

"I'll be fine. I'm going to my mom's house where they have a ridiculous security system."

"I'm coming with you," I say as I pull my phone out of my pocket and text the driver.

"*Fine,* but you're staying outside."

The driver pulls up and we step inside the car, Annaya sliding in first, of course. We sit in silence, but I can feel the tension rolling off of her in waves.

"Are you sure everything is okay?"

Annaya turns her head toward me and I can't help but take in her gorgeous features. Those sharp blue eyes that pop against her chocolatey brown hair. Her delicate cheekbones and a small nose that on anyone else would be adorable, but somehow on her, manages to be sexy. Well, and a little adorable.

"It's none of your business."

Once again, I'm about to protest, but the look she gives me has me backing down. "Okay," I reluctantly agree.

"Okay then. It's settled."

We ride the rest of the way in silence. Her breathing becomes forced and shaky the closer we get to the house.

A few minutes later, we pull into the ridiculously large drive and stop in front of the huge house. Annaya bolts out of the car and up the stairs. I follow her, stopping short of the front door as per her request.

I wait outside for a few minutes. I hear some yelling, which has my entire body on alert. Then I hear a loud crashing noise and glass shattering. There's no fucking way I'm staying out here. I kick down the door in no time and rush toward the yelling.

I have no idea what I expected to see, but I'm not prepared for the scene spread out before me.

Annaya is on one side of the living room, a shattered lamp off to one side. It looks like it was thrown at her, just missing her head. Her mother is on the other side of the room wearing a short nightgown and a silk robe, swaying unsteadily on her feet almost like she's drunk.

The woman is holding a vase in her hand, ready to toss it into the wall as well. Annaya has her hands out in front of her as if to calm the crying, angry woman across the room.

Seeing me walk in, Annaya shoots me a warning glance and barely shakes her head back and forth, telling me not to interfere.

Yeah, fuck that.

I take a step into the room, heading toward Elaine, who promptly hurls the vase in my direction. It doesn't even come close, and the momentum of her throw causes her to stumble.

Oh yeah, this woman is totally drunk.

"Mom!" Annaya rushes over to her side, kneeling down to inspect her mother to make sure she's okay.

"Don't fucking call me that!" she slurs. Annaya looks hurt for a brief second, I almost miss it, but she schools over her face again. "It's all your fault, all your fault!" Elaine bellows.

"You don't mean that."

"I do! I do! I..." The woman breaks down in a sob and Annaya holds her close as if she's the mother comforting her child. "I miss her so much. I miss her every day."

A brief flash of Annaya at the cemetery pops into my mind. Again, I wonder who died and what she meant to this family.

"I know." Annaya whispers soothing things into her mom's hair while rubbing her back. I've never seen her be so gentle.

I stand there like an idiot, not sure what to do.

Finally, Annaya looks up at me. Defeat swims in her eyes and I get a rare glimpse of the girl behind the façade. "Eli, could you maybe put some water on for tea? The kitchen is through there." She lifts her hand off of her mom's back and points to a door on the other side of the living room.

I nod and head out, grateful for something to do. Once in the kitchen, I see an electric tea kettle on the counter and fill it up with water, switching the flip on.

A few minutes later, Annaya walks into the kitchen. Her entire demeanor has changed. She's quiet, tentative almost, with her shoulders slumped and head down.

"Thanks," she murmurs as she grabs a mug from one of the cabinets. "I put her to bed. I'll get her Xanax and bring her the tea and then we can go."

"Is it a good idea to give her Xanax while she's loaded?"

Dammit. I shouldn't have said anything. I'm sure she's going to snap at me and tell me to back the hell off or not tell her what to do.

Instead, she just shrugs.

"Probably not, but it's the only thing that calms her down when she's like this. It's better than calling my dad."

Annaya grabs the bottle of pills and tea and heads upstairs.

From where I'm standing, I can see down a hallway up on the second floor. I see her back out of one of the bedrooms upstairs and close the door.

She rests her forehead on the closed door and places her hand on the wood next to her head. Annaya looks totally and completely worn out emotionally, on top of physically with the long day she's had at work.

I watch her straighten up and wipe away a few tears from her eyes. *Fuck.* Seeing her cry does something to me.

Annaya takes a deep breath and shakes it off. Literally. She shakes her head back and forth while shaking her arms and hands out at her sides. I see her square her shoulders and hold her head up, making her way down the hall toward the stairs.

I wonder how many times she's done this. How long has she been alone?

"Ready?" she asks when she gets to the door. I nod and follow her out.

When she gets in the car, Annaya pulls her knees up to her chest, wrapping her arms around them. She lays her head down over her arms, facing the window.

I can tell she's hurting, lost in her thoughts. I don't know what to do with it. I can meet her wit for wit, I can ignore her sass, and I can be firm with her when she's defiant, but this? This is uncharted territory.

"Are you going to tell me what happened in there?"

"Why do you even care?" She's trying to lash out at me, but her tone betrays her. It's less sharp and more apathetic.

"I care." I don't tell her how much I care. Way too fucking much, that's for sure, but I'm in too deep now.

We sit in silence and then she takes a deep, cleansing breath and turns her head in my direction, still resting on her arms.

She doesn't look me in the eyes, but rather past me, out my window. "I had an older sister." It's barely above a whisper. I have to lean a little closer to hear. "She was two years older than me," Annaya continues. "Alysa. It means, 'princess.'"

I wince, understanding why she hated my nickname for her.

"Alysa was always sick. A rare autoimmune disorder. She was in and out of the hospital all the time. I started donating blood when I was five. I had my first spinal tap when I was eight."

"Jesus Christ."

"You remember that movie, 'My Sister's Keeper?'"

I nod, vaguely remembering seeing a trailer about some sick kid and the family having a second kid to basically harvest her organs or some shit.

Annaya chuckles bitterly. "I related to that on a fucking *visceral* level. Did you know my name means, 'guardian, protector, defender?'"

Shit.

"I always knew what my purpose was. And that was okay, as long as I felt like I was contributing to the family, you know? Alysa was doing well for a while, almost a whole year went by without a stay in the hospital. Then one day, she collapsed. We rushed her to the ER. Both of her kidneys were failing, and fast. She needed one of mine, and the doctors assured me I could live basically a normal life with one kidney."

"How old were you?"

"Ten."

"Shit," I grunt. *What the hell?*

She just nods.

"It turns out I had Leukemia. What a disappointment I turned out to be, huh?"

My heart drops to my gut and I long to wrap her up in my arms. I finally understand why this fundraiser is so important to her.

"We didn't catch it very early because without needing to donate blood or bone marrow, I didn't have any reason to go to the doctor."

I can't stand not touching her, comforting her in some way. I rest my hand on her back and rub small circles over her shoulders and neck. She doesn't jerk away. In fact, she seems to relax a little at my touch.

"I wasn't a viable candidate for kidney donation. My parents flew me out to Seattle Children's Hospital where some of the best surgeons and oncologists are. One of their friends had a cousin out there who met me at the airport and took me to my appointments."

"Wait, they didn't go with you?"

"They had two broken kids. It was easier for them to stay home with Alysa and find her a kidney. They told me the doctors were going to do their thing with or without them, which makes sense."

I don't know what makes me angrier – her parents not going with her for what must have been terrifying and painful treatments or the fact that she doesn't see what's so fucked up about it.

"Alysa died while I was in Seattle. I didn't even know about it until two weeks later. I... I didn't get to go to her funeral."

She squeezes her eyes shut, steeling herself against the onslaught of emotions. When she opens them again, her expression is blank. How long has my Annaya kept her secrets and sorrows locked up?

"So, yeah. I went into remission a few months after Alysa died and came home. My parents were never the same. I mean, obviously. You don't just get over the death of a child. My dad threw himself into work and my mom threw herself into the bottom of a bottle."

"I'm sorry," I say lamely. I have so many questions, so many things I want to say to her, but she's exhausted. There will be time to talk about all of this later, I'll make sure of it.

Annaya shrugs. "It is what it is. My parents took care of me the best way they could. I was given a credit card, a trust fund, the best education, the finest tutors, everything. I'm thankful, I really am. Fuck. Sorry. I don't know why I told you all of that."

"Hey, I asked, didn't I?"

"Yeah, but I'm sure you didn't sign up for my entire life story."

"Thanks for telling me anyway." I smile at her. She looks so vulnerable as a shy, uncertain smile pulls at one side of her mouth.

Fuck it.

I unbuckle my seatbelt before unbuckling hers and pull her onto my lap. She tenses at first, but then she melts into my embrace. I wrap my arms around her and she presses her face into my chest. I feel her tears soaking through my shirt.

I kiss the top of her head. "It's okay, Annaya. I've got you. I've got you, baby girl."

She stays in my lap the rest of the way to her apartment. When she untangles herself from my arms, I immediately miss her body curled up into mine. It felt right. It felt like home. I know she felt it, too.

Chapter 9

Eli

I follow Annaya up to the apartment and watch as she tries to gather herself. She paces around the kitchen, grabs a bottle of water, sets it down without drinking it, then checks her phone.

"Shit!"

"What is it? What's wrong?"

"I missed the final walkthrough of the venue. It's already three. I need to get over there and see if I can do a quick run through. Oh, and check on the flowers, call the caterers, go over the menu one more time..."

I see her spinning out of control. Joining her in the kitchen, I pull her into my arms. She's shaking, and I can feel her heart pounding in her chest.

How is she even standing after today? After this week? It's all too much and I can feel her starting to fray at the edges. I want to be the one to hold her together. I want to be the one she comes to when it's all too much.

She fists my shirt and I think she might push me away, but instead, she pulls me closer.

"I've got you, Annaya. It's okay. You've already gone over the menu three times. You called about the flowers yesterday. You've poured your heart and soul into this. I've seen you worry over the details for weeks now. It's all going to come together, Annaya. You've worked so hard."

"But... but the venue..."

"Can you have your contact send you photos? There's no reason you need to leave here again today. You've had such a long day, sweetheart."

She's silent for a few minutes, just soaking up this moment in my arms.

"Yeah. That's a good idea. I can get her to send me photos."

I feel the weight lift from her shoulders, her muscles releasing tension, her soft body relaxing into mine. My chest puffs out a little with pride knowing I had a helpful idea, one that brought her a little peace.

She releases her grip on my shirt and makes a move toward her phone. I reluctantly let her go, but then I see her stumble a little on her feet. She closes her eyes for a second and sways. I scoop her up in my arms and walk her over to the couch.

"Are you okay, Annaya? Look at me, what's wrong?"

I'm trying to keep my tone neutral but inside I'm panicking. What if she gets sick again? She's been in remission for years, but that stuff can come back, right? I can't lose her, I just found her.

As if reading my mind, Annaya reaches out and puts a hand on my chest.

"I'm okay, Eli. I'm just a little light-headed is all."

"Have you eaten today? Had any water?"

"Ummm..."

"Shit, Annaya, you have to take care of yourself!" I snap.

I see the hurt in her eyes.

I scrub my hands down my face, trying to get my shit together. No one has the power to unravel me as quickly as this woman, but I need to be strong right now for her.

"I'm sorry, baby. I'm just worried about you. You've been working yourself to the bone. Let me feed you and get you some water. Just stay there."

She nods her head and lets me gently guide her so she's laying down on the couch. I slip her shoes off and pull a blanket over her.

Walking over to the kitchen, I grab the water bottle she abandoned on the counter and hand it to her.

"Drink this while I make us a late lunch, okay?"

She nods again. It's like that's the only thing she has the energy to do.

Annaya doesn't have much in her kitchen, but I manage to make us some stir-fry. I walk it over to her and she's on her laptop. I give her a stern look, and she smiles sweetly up at me.

My heart just about stops. She's so fucking beautiful. Maybe after today, I'll get to see more of her smiles.

"I just got the pictures of the venue emailed to me."

"Can I see?"

She scoots over and turns the laptop toward me as I set the bowls of stir-fry on the coffee table in front of us.

She scrolls through the photos and I'm stunned. Sure, I followed her to all of her appointments, listened while she told the board her vision, and watched as she picked out tablecloths and lights and décor, but I didn't understand how it would look all put together.

It's truly stunning. It's elegant and sophisticated but not gaudy. I know she wants the main focus to be on the charity work, but that still means she has to do a lot of work on the ambiance.

I may not know anything about event planning or charity fundraisers, but I know Annaya is talented as fuck. And she did all of this by herself. She's amazing. Incredible, really.

"So... what do you think?"

I look over at her and she's nervously chewing her lip, searching my eyes for approval.

"Annaya, it's amazing. I never would have pictured all the details coming together, but I can tell you had a plan all along. It's flawless. Tomorrow is going to be amazing."

"Yeah? You really think so?" I've never seen her insecure like this, especially about her work.

"Definitely, Annaya. This is incredible. You're incredible."

She beams up at me, hitting me with a brilliant smile, like nothing I've ever seen on her or anyone. It takes all the air out of my lungs. I swear my heart stops beating. I didn't think she could possibly get any more beautiful, but this look right here... she's perfect.

"Thank you."

She keeps smiling at me, basking in my approval. I didn't realize it meant so much to her, but I guess after hearing her story, she probably doesn't get much approval from her parents. I aim to shower her with more love and compliments than she can handle.

Annaya looks away from me, but her smile still lingers. Closing the laptop and setting it on the coffee table, she looks at the bowl of stir-fry.

"You made this?"

I nod.

"In my kitchen?"

I laugh. "Yeah, did you know you can make more than smoothies and avocado toast in that massive kitchen of yours?"

She rolls her eyes but laughs with me as she digs in.

"Mmmm...oh my God this is so *goooood*!" she says with a mouth full of rice and veggies. It's too fucking cute.

I grin at her as she inhales the food. I like providing for her, taking care of her. I think I could spend my whole life right here next to her.

And then I remember the ranch.

How could I forget the whole reason I'm here? To make money to save the family ranch. My whole life is back in Montana. I look over at Annaya and think maybe my whole life is here, too.

"Watcha thinkin' about over there? You look very broody."

I shake my thoughts. I still have a month with Annaya. No use worrying about all of that stuff now.

"Nothing, sweetheart."

I sit back and relax on the couch, and to my surprise, Annaya curls up next to me. I grab the blanket and drape it over her before wrapping my arm around her waist and pulling her closer. She rests her head on my chest and sighs.

"Thank you, Eli. For today. For helping with Elaine, and work, cooking me dinner, taking care of me. No one's ever... I mean, just... thanks."

She looks up at me and I know I'm gone. Done. Game over.

I love her. I love her so fucking much.

I bend down and kiss her forehead before resting my forehead on hers. I want to do so much more, but this will have to do for now.

"Thank you for letting me take care of you, sweetheart." I kiss her forehead one last time and then tuck her head into my chest, resting my chin on top of her head.

We stay like that for who knows how long, but then Annaya suddenly jerks awake, hopping off of the couch and taking all the warmth with her.

"A tux! Oh my God, I forgot to get you a tux!"

"It's okay, I brought one. Now get your sexy ass back here and keep me warm."

"You have a tux?" She looks completely shocked, and I've got to say, I like that look on her.

I smile. "Yeah, just because I live on a ranch doesn't mean I can't also have a tux. You never know when you might need one. I figured when I came out here, I might need one."

"Oh. Well, good."

"Glad that's settled," I say. "Now, are you going to get back here?" I grin at her.

She tries to hide her smile as she slips back under the blanket and curls into my side, right where she belongs. We watch some stupid reality TV show, but honestly, I'd watch anything as long as it meant she'll stay here with me forever.

I'm so lost for this girl and she has no idea.

Chapter 10

Annaya

I wake up to the smell of bacon. I don't think that's ever happened to me.

Am I having a stroke?

Wait, no that would be a burnt toast smell.

The last thing I remember is cuddling with Eli on the couch.

He was so good to me yesterday, which is confusing. I've been kind of a bitch to him, but I was so stressed about the fundraiser and then that whole situation with my mom... I didn't have the strength to keep him at arm's length anymore. If he wanted to feed me and tuck me in, he could.

He must have carried me to bed last night. I look down and see I'm wearing a tank top and panties – much like the first morning Eli and I shared together.

Apparently, he also undressed me last night.

That should make me upset, but I only feel a rush of heat straight to my core. I know nothing can happen between us again, but damn was he incredible.

Get it together. Today is the big day and I don't need those kinds of distractions. I put on a robe and pad out to the kitchen.

"Mornin' beautiful," Eli says while flipping over bacon in a pan, shirtless, of course. How is that even safe?

There's no denying the heat that flashes through me, settling between my thighs. He's gorgeous.

I shake the thoughts from my head. "Uh, hi. What is all of this?"

There's a pitcher of orange juice on the kitchen table, along with a bowl of fresh fruit, a pot of coffee, and plates set out. Eli flips the last piece of bacon onto a plate and gets to work cracking eggs in the same pan that the bacon just came from.

"Breakfast," he says with a smirk.

I roll my eyes.

"Yes, I realize it's breakfast, but I mean...how did you get all this food? And why?"

He stops tending to the eggs and looks up at me. God, those hazel eyes. His brow furrows slightly as he searches my face for something.

Then he snaps out of it and smiles again. "I had some groceries delivered last night after you went to bed. As for the why...sweetheart, it's for you. Today's the big day, I want to make sure you have a good start, plenty of protein and whatnot."

"Oh..." My breath gets caught in my throat and I feel stupid tears burn in the back of my eyes. I look down at my lap.

What is my problem? Why is breakfast food making me cry?

I clear my throat and try to get my shit together. "I can pay you back for the groceries, that really wasn't necessary."

Eli finishes the scrambled eggs and plates them, carrying the last part of our feast over to the table. He pulls out a chair for me and motions for me to sit down. My body starts moving toward him before my brain even catches up.

He pushes the chair in once I sit down, and he bends down so his lips are right next to my ear.

"Let me take care of you, Annaya. I want to do this for you." He kisses my temple and my stomach flips.

Why is he being so nice to me?

Eli sits across from me and starts serving up breakfast.

"What all do we have to do today?" He asks. I'm thankful for the topic of work to talk about instead of trying to figure out these confusing feelings I'm starting to have.

"Today is all about crisis management," I reply. "Technically, I don't have to be at the fundraiser until four to make final adjustments and walk through security details, but there will be several disasters before then. My schedule is cleared up for whenever the shit hits the fan."

"Oh? Like what?"

"Who knows?" I laugh. "The chef getting the flu, finding out the keynote speaker is allergic to the flowers on the tables, the building erupting in fire... anything is possible. I kind of like this part though. I like figuring out contingency plans."

"You have a contingency plan for if the building catches on fire?" he asks with an amused grin.

"Yup. I'm going to crawl into bed with a bottle of vodka."

Eli bursts out laughing, and it might be my new favorite sound. I don't think I've ever heard him laugh before, full-on, belly laughing.

"Is it terrible that I almost want the building to catch on fire so I can join you in bed with a bottle of vodka?"

I choke on a bite of eggs and feel the heat all over my face. Eli laughs again as I take a swig of orange juice to get myself under control.

"You might not have to set a building on fire to get me in bed."

I don't know why I said that. I have no idea what came over me. *God. What was I thinking?*

I look up at Eli and his eyes have gone dark. He flares his nostrils and stares at me. I can practically feel him undressing me with his eyes.

"Jesus, Annaya. You can't say shit like that to me."

"Oh? But it's okay for you to say it to me?" I tease. I don't know where this boldness with him is coming from.

"I don't think it means the same thing to you as it does to me."

I'm not sure what he means by that. Surely he doesn't mean...no, he can't possibly *like* me, right?

The tension has become weird in here, so I stand up and clear the dishes from the table. I grab my mug and turn to the coffee maker to pour myself another cup.

I feel his heat on my back before I even reach for the coffee pot. Eli places his hands on my hips, and I grip the counter in front of me. It's the same position we were in that first morning in this kitchen, the same place even.

He bends down, his hot breath blowing across my skin and setting my nerves on fire. His lips graze up my neck and settle on the shell of my ear.

"I put you in the same clothes as the first time we were in this kitchen together. Part of me was hoping for a repeat performance." He scrapes his teeth on my ear and I moan. "But I see you decided to throw on a robe this time. Does that mean you want me to back off?"

He nuzzles my neck and I melt into him, arching my back and pressing my ass into his already hardening cock. I untie my robe in front, letting the sides fall open in invitation.

Eli doesn't waste a second. He slides the robe off my left shoulder, kissing each inch of skin as it is exposed. Soon the robe is in a pile at my feet and Eli's hands make their way under my tank top, just like they did that first morning.

He moves his fingers so slowly up my ribcage and back down my tummy, all the while sucking my neck and shoulders.

One hand moves lower, cupping my pussy over my panties. I groan and jerk my hips.

"Fuck, baby, are you wet for me?"

I can't even form words as one hand continues its slow exploration of my skin and the other massages my clit through the thin fabric.

"Mmmm... more, please..."

Eli growls and slips his hand underneath my panties, sliding a thick finger through my folds, up my slit.

"Ah! Yes!" I buck my hips back and grind against his cock.

"Annaya," he groans into my neck.

His finger swirls around my tight little ball of nerves and I throw my head back, resting it on his shoulder. Eli's other hand creeps up the side of my body and grasps my left breast, kneading the sensitive flesh. He flicks his thumb over my nipple and pinches it, sending a wave of pleasure straight to my core.

"Fuck, baby, I feel you gushing for me."

Eli shoves two fingers into my entrance and I cry out. He thrusts in and out of me with his thick digits while his palm grinds against my clit. His other hand slides up my chest until his fingers wrap around my throat, applying the lightest of pressure.

"Yes! Oh, fuck, Eli..."

He tightens his grip around my neck slightly and my pussy releases another wave of wetness on his hand as I grind my ass into his hard cock.

"You like that, baby girl?"

He curls his fingers up inside of me, hitting that most sensitive spot. It's all too much, my body humming with pleasure, excitement, and need.

His calloused fingers continue to thrust and rub against my G-spot while his palm grinds my clit. My pulse jumps against his other hand wrapped around my neck. I feel like I've been on the exquisite edge of an orgasm for hours with the way Eli is working my body.

He withdraws his fingers from my hole and slides them up my slit, blurring them furiously over my clit, winding me tighter and tighter with each touch.

I moan wildly, the sound nearly feral as Eli brings me right up to the edge.

He pinches my clit and I snap, convulsing in his arms. He lets go of my throat right as my orgasm hits, flooding my system with oxygen, making me feel like I might explode with pleasure all over again.

Eli continues to stroke my clit in lazy circles, drawing out my orgasm as I shake and finally come back down to earth.

He takes his hands out of my panties and spins me around so we're facing each other. Then, Eli sucks my cum off his fingers. It's so goddamn dirty.

He grabs the back of my neck with one hand and pulls me into a punishing kiss. I taste myself on him and it gets me so hot all over again.

"Don't you taste delicious?" he growls into my mouth.

I nod, still lost in the fog of pleasure.

He rests his forehead on mine, we're both still breathing heavily. In a bold move, I reach between us, into his sweatpants, and pull out his hard cock.

Eli hisses and flares his nostrils. I stroke his thickness, slowly at first, but then I pick up my speed. His one hand is still gripping the back of my neck, and his other hand squeezes my ass. With his forehead still on mine, I can feel all of his muscles tensing, feel the ecstasy coursing through his veins.

"Yes, baby, just like that, shit," he groans.

I pump two more times and feel him spray his hot cum across my belly with a roar. He drops his head to rest on the crook of my shoulder, both hands circling my waist and drawing me in for a hug.

As we both come down from that intense high, I start to freak out.

What does this mean? We can't be together; he's leaving in a month. I have no idea what I'm doing. I don't need this distraction. What the hell was I thinking?

Then my phone rings.

Saved by the bell.

Eli reluctantly steps back, giving me space to grab my phone.

It's the caterer. Of course.

I grab a washcloth and wipe off the mess Eli left on me, then put my phone on speaker as I rush to my room to get cleaned up.

Twenty minutes later, Eli and I are dressed and ready to meet with the caterer to discuss an alternative for some spinach dip he can no longer make because of the E-coli outbreak that was just announced this morning.

I usually love this last-minute stuff, working out the kinks and facing challenges head-on while on a strict time crunch. But right now, all I want to do is ask Eli about what's happening between us.

Chapter 11

Eli

Six hours later and I can't stop thinking about Annaya. I didn't plan on anything happening in the kitchen this morning. I really just wanted to make her a nice breakfast since I knew it was going to be a long day for her.

But then we got to flirting and one thing led to another and when I touched her, I couldn't stop. I had to feel her, had to have some part of me inside of her again.

I love watching her cum. Love that moment when her body takes over and she lets the world around her fall away. She's so goddamn sexy.

I shake my head of those thoughts. Now is not the time to be getting hard. Not in this tux. I'm waiting by the front door for Annaya to make her grand appearance before we officially head off to the fundraiser.

Just like Annaya predicted, there was a lot of crisis management today, which she handled like a fucking queen. She was decisive and communicative and gracious. I love seeing her in her element. I only wish her parents could see her like this too. I have no doubt they'd be proud of all her hard work. I'm sure they'll see it tonight.

The clicking of heels on the hardwood floor draws my attention back to the present.

Annaya stands before me like the radiant goddess she is.

My eyes sweep up her body, taking in every inch of her. She's wearing a deep blue silk gown that hugs her curves and drapes over her elegantly. Her silky side-swept hair flows over one shoulder, just begging me to run my fingers through it.

Annaya's brilliant blue eyes are lined in black and framed with thick, long lashes, making them pop all the more against her skin. She's so beautiful it almost hurts to look at her.

I see her worry the corner of her lip – her luscious lip, lined with a dark red lipstick.

"That bad, huh?" She tries for a joke, but I can tell she's pretty self-conscience in her formal wear. I realize I've just been staring at her wordlessly for the last two minutes.

I clear my throat. "Annaya, you are stunning. I mean, you are always beautiful, but this..." I look her up and down again and can't seem to find adequate words. "You're just... fuck, baby. You're gorgeous."

I'm rewarded with a blush and a genuine smile. My heart melts for her. She's so strong and yet she lets me see some of her insecurities, so I can cover them with my own strength.

"Thank you. God, Eli, you can really wear a tux, huh?"

It's her turn to look me up and down.

"I can clean up when the right occasion comes along," I wink at her and hold out my arm. She tucks her hand into the crook of my elbow and we head downstairs to the driver.

***

People are starting to show up and Annaya is ever the gracious and beautiful event planner. She stays behind the scenes, checks up on the different moving pieces, and then makes time to do a lap around the lobby to greet people as they walk in. I know part of her reason for coming back out to the lobby is to see when her parents get here.

Someone comes up and whispers into Annaya's ear and she turns on her heel, off to solve another crisis no doubt. I keep an eye on her while sweeping the perimeter. I have a bad feeling about tonight.

Not anything to do with the event itself – God knows, Annaya has worked her sexy little ass off to make everything perfect. It's more a gut feeling about Annaya's safety. This is the perfect place for something terrible to happen.

I already met with the security team Annaya hired. We've gone over the layout, the cameras, the exits, and the potential weak spots. They are a solid team, and as with everything tonight, Annaya did an excellent job picking out the best of the best.

The mingling/cocktail hour is over and almost everyone has shown up. People are heading toward their assigned seats and dinner is about to begin. I make my way over to my seat, next to Annaya. Mr. and Mrs. Moretti's seats are across the table, still empty.

Rage and sadness mix in my gut and I look over at Annaya to see how she's taking it all in. She smiles and looks relieved to see me. I lean over and kiss her temple, scooting my chair closer to hers so I can hold her hand.

"I'm sure they're going to be here any minute," Annaya says, nodding toward the empty seats. "Presley probably had a late meeting or something. They said they'd be here though."

She seems to be saying it more to herself than to me. They better fucking show up for their daughter. I don't need another reason to hate them.

I put my arm around her shoulders and pull her into my side.

"This night is perfect, Annaya. Everyone has been talking about the décor and how much they love the music. Word on the street is the menu looks to die for."

"Yeah?" She looks up at me.

"Yes, sweetheart. I've been spying on everyone with your security team. I was going to punch anyone who had a bad word to say, but so far, it's all been good." I grin at her and she laughs.

The first course is served, and Annaya and I chat with the other couple seated at our table. Her smile is easy and she keeps up her end of the conversation like a pro, but I can feel the tension pouring out of her small body each minute her parents don't show up.

She starts bouncing her leg underneath the table and I rest my hand on top of her knee to calm her down. I lean in and graze her ear with my lips.

"Take a deep breath, baby girl. Don't let them ruin tonight. You're a fucking rock star and you deserve to enjoy this event."

I look at her out of the corner of my eye and see her nod before taking a few steadying breaths. She looks over her shoulder at me and mouths, "thank you."

Halfway through the second course, I see Presley making his way toward the table. He's way underdressed in khakis and a blazer. He looks like he just came from some good ol' boys club meeting. If he took any time to look over the invitation or research the venue, he would know this is clearly a black-tie event.

Annaya doesn't seem to notice or care how he's dressed. Her whole face lights up and I swear my heart cracks in two knowing he's going to disappoint her. There's no way this ends well.

"Dad!" She jumps up and lifts her arms up for a hug. He sticks his hand out for a handshake.

Is he fucking serious right now?

Annaya takes it all in stride, shaking his hand.

"I'm so glad you made it tonight, dad." He gives her a stern look. "I mean, Presley." He nods.

I grit my teeth thinking about how both her parents told her to call them by their first names. This girl has been denied love for so long, but I'll make up for it.

"Yes, well...I didn't think it'd be quite so formal. Or so many people."

"Oh, did you not get the invitation?"

"I did, I did. Must've misread it."

Annaya nods, totally buying his bullshit. Not me.

"Where's Elaine?"

"She is under the weather this evening, I'm afraid."

Aka drunk and passed out.

"Oh." Annaya slumps her shoulders a bit. "That's too bad. I got her favorite flowers for the centerpieces – remember how she's always liked these mariposa lilies? Maybe you could take one of the arrangements home for her?"

Presley grunts in response. Actually grunts. At his own daughter. It's painful to watch. She just wants his love or at least some acknowledgment, yet he can barely even talk to her.

He sits down, and she comes back to her seat. I grab her hand under the table and give it a squeeze. She laces her fingers in mine and squeezes me back.

We make uneasy conversation while the last course of dinner is served. The other couple at the table can clearly sense the tension in our newest table member. Presley keeps checking his watch and looks annoyed.

"So," I clear my throat. "Annaya really did an amazing job planning everything, don't you think, Mr. Moretti?"

Annaya leans over and whispers, "You don't have to do this."

I just squeeze her hand again and wait for her dad to respond.

"Mmhm, yes. It's nice."

"You're the event planner?" the other lady at our table asks.

Annaya nods.

"How wonderful! Oh, I just love the décor, it's so tasteful and elegant but not overbearing. So many of these things just turn out to be a way for people to flaunt their money and pat themselves on the back, but I can tell this isn't going to be like that at all."

Annaya blushes and thanks the woman. They chat a bit about the chef and vendors, and Annaya hands out her business card. That's my girl. Keep that business coming in.

Her dad doesn't say another word.

When the servers start clearing the plates from the last course, someone goes up to the podium to introduce the speaker. Presley scoots his chair back and stands up.

"Where are you going?" Annaya asks.

"Sorry, I am late for a previous engagement. I didn't think this would take up the whole evening."

No. No way is he leaving. It's barely been an hour.

"Oh... uh..." I can tell Annaya is trying to remain neutral, professional.

"Surely you can stay another hour, can't you Mr. Moretti? Your daughter put a lot of effort into this evening. I understand it means a lot to your family."

Uh oh. From the look in his eyes, I've clearly gone too far.

"And what do you know about my family, *Eli*?"

"Not much, sir. I was just saying—"

Annaya squeezes my hand and rubs her thumb across my knuckles.

"It's okay, Presley. I understand. Thank you for stopping by tonight."

He grunts again, still eyeing me.

"I already wrote the check. I'll hand it in on my way out."

Annaya gapes at him as he walks away, but she quickly pulls it together. The other couple at our table does their best to pretend they didn't just witness her asshole of a father.

The keynote speaker gets up and Annaya excuses herself to the bathroom. I wait a minute and follow her out.

I see her leaning against a wall at the end of a long hallway. I jog up to her, wanting to pull her into my arms, but she holds out a hand to stop me.

"I'm okay, Eli. I... shit."

She takes a deep breath and closes her eyes. I step closer to her and put a hand on her shoulder. She flinches from my touch, and I try not to let it hurt.

"Please, just... give me some space. I'm okay."

"I'm not okay," I tell her, honestly.

Her eyes snap open and she looks at me with such concern. "What's wrong?"

She really has no idea how important she is to me.

"Your dad! I mean, how can he just... treat you that way? I can't imagine anyone overlooking you. You're incredible. You're all I see."

I need to touch her. Fucking *need* it.

"Can I hold you, Annaya? I think we both need it."

She stares at me, fighting back tears. Finally, she nods. I wrap my arms around her and kiss her temple. I rest my forehead on top of her head and whisper into her hair the words she needs to hear, the ones I need to tell her.

"I'm so proud of you, Annaya. You are an incredible woman, and anyone would be lucky to have you as a daughter. I'm so sorry your parents couldn't be here like you needed them to be tonight, or shit, like you needed them to be there for your whole life. But you're so strong, God, Annaya, I..."

Shit.

I almost told her I love her. It's too soon, I know.

She clings to me and I feel her tiny body shaking. Suddenly, she pushes me away and ducks underneath my arms. Her eyes are rimmed in red and she sniffles as she runs down the hall toward the back exit.

"Annaya! Wait!" I call out as I run after her.

"I just need some space, please!"

She opens the door to the alley, and I see a hand in a black glove grab her arm and yank her the rest of the way outside.

Adrenaline spikes my blood and I sprint toward the door, every one of my protective instincts clicking into place.

I burst out into the alley in time to see Annaya being shoved into a car.

Chapter 12

Annaya

Eli told me he was proud of me. It broke something and healed something inside of me at the same time and suddenly it was all too much.

The stress of the night, the months of planning, the utter disappointment when my dad showed up and tossed money at me without a second thought as to why I really wanted him here tonight.

And then there's Eli. He stood up for me. He calmed me down. He supported me. He was perfect. And too much. I couldn't breathe.

I panicked and ran out into the alley – into the hands of a large, terrifying man.

"Ah, we've been waiting for you, Annaya. Nice of you to make our jobs easier."

The man jerks me toward a car.

No, no, no, I have to be here for the fundraiser...

I know, I should probably be scared for my life, but all I can think of is how hard I've worked for this night. Now the only memories I'll have are my dad being a gigantic asshole and getting kidnapped. That is if I live to have any memories at all.

Oh, fuck.

The gravity of my situation just sank in.

"Wait! Stop! You can't..."

He grips me tighter and shoves my head into the side of the car, effectively shutting me up while another man secures my wrists with a zip tie.

The door I just came out of opens again and I see Eli standing there, gun drawn, right before I'm shoved into the car.

The car door slams shut and the car roars down the alley.

"They never told us you were so pretty," the masked man says as he grabs my face in his hands.

I try biting him and he slaps me.

"Tsk, tsk, Annaya. Now I'm going to have to gag you." He grabs a cloth and shoves it in my mouth before covering my lips with duct tape.

I strain against the zip tie and try not to choke on the cloth trapped in my mouth. As cliché as it is, my life spreads out before me, but not as a reel of memories.

It's like my body is remembering all of my most intense moments – the loneliness of my time battling cancer at Seattle Children's, the rage when my parents refused to acknowledge me over and over, the anger and sadness when I learned of Alysa's death... and more recently, the intense pleasure I have when I'm with Eli, the love we share.

What? *Love.*

Shit.

I buck my head up and smash the guy sitting next to me right in the nose. I hear a satisfying snap.

"Fucking cunt!" he yells as blood gushes out of his face.

"What the hell is going on back there?" the driver asks. It's just the two of them.

"She broke my fucking nose!"

The driver laughs.

"Hey, fuck you, Matt, you wanna sit back here with her?"

"No names, you moron!" the driver yells, reaching back to hit the guy beside me.

The idiots slap at each other while slowly driving down the alley. While they're distracted, I wiggle my hands around and flick my wrist against the door handle, assuming it's locked.

It isn't. I fall backward out of the car and roll off to the side.

"SHIT!" they both scream as the driver slams on the brakes.

I kick my shoes off and struggle to my feet, running toward Eli, who is now sprinting in my direction.

"Get down!" he yells at me. I drop to my hands and knees right before he fires in the direction of the car, clipping the side mirror on the right side of the vehicle. "That was a warning shot, motherfuckers. If you come near her, I will not hesitate to put a bullet in your head."

I start crawling toward Eli once again, looking over my shoulder to make sure they aren't coming after me. The driver puts his hands up, but Broken-Nose-McGee wrestles with the gun at his hip.

"Dude, this isn't worth getting killed for, man," The driver says. "The bounty isn't even that high."

I make it to Eli, who shoves me behind him after sweeping my body for any serious injuries. I duck behind him, making myself as small as possible on the ground.

"What bounty?" Eli yells.

Neither man speaks.

Eli shoots off the other side mirror.

"I won't ask again. What bounty?"

"There's a bounty on her head. Annaya Moretti. I can't believe we were the first ones to get to her. There's gotta be like ten other people looking for her."

"Shut the fuck up," the other guy hisses. "If we're not gonna get paid, we can at least try and get out of here alive."

They scramble back into the car and peel away. Eli stands there with his gun trained on the car until they're out of sight. Then, he turns and drops to his knees.

"Annaya, are you hurt?" His eyes are swimming with all kinds of emotions, the bravado of protecting me now replaced with fear at what could have happened.

I lift my head so he sees the duct tape on my mouth.

"Shit, sweetheart. I'm so sorry, this is going to sting." He removes the duct tape and I spit out the cloth, gagging a little.

"Jesus Christ, Annaya. Are you hurt?" he asks again.

I shake my head no. I honestly can't feel anything right now.

He leans over and cuts the zip tie off, rubbing my wrists to get rid of the red mark. Eli holds my hands in his and searches all over for cuts and scrapes before scooping me up in his arms.

"I'm so sorry, baby. Fuck, I'm so sorry," he says over and over again.

"I'm okay, Eli, I'm okay,"

"Shh, don't talk. Let me take care of you. I've got you now. I'm never letting go."

Between my dad, the kidnapping, the cut on my head from being slammed against the car, and my huge revelation that I *love* Eli, it's all too much. My vision starts to tunnel.

"Annaya?" It sounds so far away. I feel a slight prick of pain as Eli touches the cut on my head. "Fuck, baby, I thought you said you weren't hurt..."

"I'm okay..." I mumble before passing out.

Chapter 13

Eli

I have never known fear like that. Seeing Annaya being kidnaped triggered something deep inside. I was going to kill those motherfuckers.

As I raced toward the car, Annaya stumbled out. I have no idea how she managed it, but of course, my girl was strong enough to outsmart those idiots. When they said there was a bounty on her head I knew what I had to do. It was the only option, really.

I would have asked her opinion, but she passed out right after I saw a huge cut on her head. It looked like they smacked her up against the car, and I regret not killing at least one of them.

After getting back to Annaya's place, I cleaned her up and got her changed into an old shirt of mine. I tucked her in and began making plans to take her back home with me to Montana. No one would look for her there.

It's around two in the morning now. I just got done booking flights for us after creating a fake email and opening a new credit card under a fake ID. Yeah, I still have some shady connections from when I was in the security business full time.

This will make it next to impossible to trace us. I got Annaya a fake ID too. They aren't cheap to come by, but I know a guy who owes me some favors.

I pack our bags with just the basics. Annaya can get whatever she wants when we get to Montana, I just need to make sure I get her out safely. That's my only goal right now.

Our flight leaves in three hours and I hate to wake her, but we have to get going. I'm not sure how she's going to respond to all of this, but I have no time. We have to get going so we can meet the guy with our new IDs and make it to the airport in time.

I crawl in bed next to Annaya and tuck a loose strand of hair behind her ear. She stirs but doesn't wake.

"Hey, sweetheart, we need to get going, okay?"

She blinks up at me, still half asleep.

"Eli?"

"Yeah, Annaya, I'm here."

She smiles, but tears start rolling down her cheeks.

"Oh, baby, don't cry, please don't cry, you're okay."

I kiss her forehead and wipe her tears away with my thumbs.

"Sorry, Eli, I'm... sorry, I'm confused. What happened? I was at the fundraiser..."

Her eyes pop open as she shoots up in bed. I can practically see the evening playing out in her head. I wrap my arms around her and hold her close while she processes what happened.

"I've got you. I'm here. I've got you." I rock her back and forth. "Annaya, we have to leave here, you understand that, right?"

She nods her head against my chest.

"I have a plan to keep you safe, but you have to listen to me and do what I say, okay?"

Again, her head nods. I pull back a little bit so I can look her in the eyes as I tell her this next part.

"We're leaving for the airport now. I'm taking you back to my ranch in Montana."

I hold my breath, waiting for her to protest, tell me about how she can't leave work or has to set up someone to look after her apartment, or just to fight me because that's what she's really good at.

Instead, she throws her arms around me and buries her head in my neck. My arms automatically circle around her.

"I'll go wherever you go, Eli," she whispers into the side of my neck.

Fuck, I like the sound of that.

I scoop her up and help her change into the clothes I picked out for her. She doesn't fight me at all. I do a final walk-through of her place and she never leaves my side. We walk out the door, hand in hand, and grab a taxi to JFK.

Once inside the airport, everything goes as planned. We meet my guy, board our plane, and head out to Montana.

I imagined coming back home a thousand times since taking this job a month ago, but I never pictured anything like this happening. I definitely didn't think I'd be flying incognito with a fake ID or on the run from some thug bounty hunters.

I didn't think I'd be coming home with the woman I want to marry by my side, either. And I never, in a million years, thought that woman would be Annaya Moretti.

I look over at her now, sitting next to me, facing the window. Her fingers are laced in mine. She hasn't said anything since we left her place. She also hasn't stopped touching me. Like I'm her anchor. I don't deserve her trust. I let her down only a few short hours ago, and yet here she is, flying across the country with me.

We'll have time to discuss the details later. I wouldn't be upset one bit if we never came back to New York City again. Good riddance.

Chapter 14

Annaya

I wake up in a huge, fluffy, four-poster bed. It's not the most comfortable bed I've ever been in, but something about it feels like... home. A comfort beyond the physical. Something warm that surrounds me and blankets me with familiarity, like I somehow remember this place. It's been etched in my bones, and now that I'm here, I can finally rest.

I roll over and run right into Eli.

"Morning, beautiful. Or, I guess, afternoon." He smiles down at me. He must have been awake for some time, just sitting up next to me, working on his laptop.

"Hi." I'm not sure how to communicate my new feelings of belonging.

"How are you feeling?" He puts his laptop away and turns toward me, searching my eyes with such worry. His concern is unnerving, and I still don't really know what to do with all of his attention.

"Um, I'm fine. I think."

"Look at me, Annaya."

He puts two fingers under my chin and guides my face up toward his.

"How are you? Talk to me. You've had an impossible last couple of days. Tell me what you're thinking. Please, baby."

"Honestly, Eli, I feel... I don't know. I feel safe. Is that stupid? I mean, it is, obviously. I don't even know where I am. I'm probably concussed, right? My head doesn't even hurt though. But maybe I'm still groggy. I don't know. I feel good right here, with you. So... I guess, thank you." I bury my head in his chest, unable to look him in the eye after my dumb, incoherent rant. "Never mind," I mumble into his chest.

Eli strokes my hair and kisses the top of my head.

"I feel good right here with you too, Annaya."

We stay like that for a while, but then I feel the need to wash the last twenty four hours off my skin. I could tell Eli rinsed me off last night, cleaned up my wounds, and whatnot, but I want to wash it all away. More than just the dirt and blood, I want to wash the memory of my dad, of the threats, of my old life away.

"Is the bathroom in there?" I ask, pointing to a smaller door that looks like it leads to an en suite bathroom.

"Yeah, you want to shower?"

I nod. "And I want you to join me."

Eli growls and scoops me up, heading toward the bathroom.

"Are you sure you're okay, baby?" Eli asks as he sets me down on the sink. "You hit your head really hard. I don't want to hurt you. And once I get you naked, I *will* be fucking you in that shower."

I bite my lip and pull him closer to me, capturing his lips with mine in a sweet kiss.

"Then fuck me, Eli," I whisper into his ear before licking the side of his neck.

"Goddamn, baby. You don't have to ask me twice."

He pulls the shirt off my body along with my panties.

"You're so goddamn beautiful, Annaya. I don't even know where to start."

"How about start by taking your clothes off too?" I tease.

In record time, Eli rips his clothes off and is naked before me. He really is stunning. I love his broad shoulders and defined pecs, the corded muscles in his arms, all of his strength that he uses to protect and surprisingly comfort me. And then there's his cock. His glorious monster cock that stretched me so good last time, hitting places inside of me I didn't even know existed. Without even thinking, I lick my lips.

"See something you like?"

I look up and Eli is grinning at me.

"Yeah," I say before pulling him down for a kiss.

It's just as explosive as I remember, our tongues warring for control as his hands stroke my body up and down. He cups my ass and lifts me up, walking us toward the shower, never breaking the kiss.

Only when he sets me down, do we both come up for air.

"Fuck, baby. I missed you. Missed these lips," he kisses me again, short and sweet. "Missed your skin," he kisses across my jaw, down my neck, over my collar bone. "Missed these perfect breasts," he sucks one of my breasts in his mouth while flicking the nipple on my other breast with his thumb. Everything he does drives me crazy with want, need.

"Ah, yes..." I moan.

Eli kisses lower, kneeling before me. His hands rest on my hips, guiding me backward so I'm leaning against the wall of the shower.

"I've wanted to taste your sweet cunt since that moment in the kitchen all those weeks ago."

I moan at his words, loving the dirty way he's talking to me. He nips at my hip bone and blazes a trail of kisses to my other hip bone, where he sucks and nips the skin. I feel his hands massaging my ass, then gripping lower on my thighs.

Eli guides one leg up over his shoulder, giving him complete access to my soaked pussy. I feel exposed, but not in a bad way. I should be embarrassed, but I'm not. He looks like he's about to go out of his mind with need, and I feel the same.

He turns his head and sinks his teeth into the thigh that is slung over his shoulder, kissing away the sting.

"Are you wet for me, baby?"

I nod and dig my fingers into his hair, urging him forward.

He chuckles. "You want it bad, don't you, Annaya? Want my tongue inside your juicy pussy?"

Before I can reply, he devours me.

He flattens his tongue and runs it from my entrance to my clit. Again. Again. I buck my hips and moan his name.

"So fucking delicious. Better than I dreamed."

He dives back between my legs, spearing his tongue deep inside my channel, causing my pussy walls to pulse around him and release a wave of wetness. Eli growls and I feel the vibrations echoing off every nerve in my body.

He pulls his tongue out and thrusts it back in, fucking me with his mouth while rubbing my clit with his thumb. It's almost too much, I feel myself getting close already. So close...

Eli withdraws his tongue and finger and I cry out at the loss.

"I've got you, baby. I'll always take care of you."

He licks my tight ball of nerves, drawing figure eights with his tongue, over and over. And then he slams two fingers in my hole and my body jerks, back arching off of the wall.

Eli moves his other hand from my hip to my stomach, spreading his fingers out over my tummy, keeping me pinned to the wall, while also intensifying the pressure I feel building again in my lower abdomen.

"D-don't stop, please..."

He pumps his fingers faster, curling them up and hitting my most sensitive spot. My thighs jerk together and he strokes the spot again.

"Ah, ah, too much..."

"I've got you, let go for me, cum all over my face."

He returns his attention to my clit, alternating between fast, slow, hard, and soft licks. Then, he sucks my little nub into his mouth and softly bites down. That's it. My orgasm rips through me.

"Oh fuck, Eli!" I nearly scream.

He replaces his fingers with his tongue, lapping up all of my cum as my pussy convulses around him, squeezing his tongue as he massages my walls. I can feel the stress melt off of my bones and pool in my core, dripping out of me as Eli sucks it all in.

The last of my orgasm fades and I slump against Eli. He stands up and kisses me, long and deep, slow and passionate. I taste myself on him and it's so fucking hot. He slides his hands up to my hips and I throw my arms around his neck, forcing the kiss to go deeper.

He finally breaks the kiss and nuzzles my neck, kissing my shoulder.

"Goddamn, baby. Love watching you come apart in my hands, in my mouth. Fucking beautiful."

He lifts his head and rests it on my forehead. We're both breathing heavily, sharing the same air, the same intensity.

I slide my hands down his neck, over his chest, down his well-defined abs, and grip his hard cock. He hisses and throws his head back.

"Your turn," I grin up at him.

"Shit, Annaya…"

I kneel before him and he puts his hands on the wall in front of him to steady himself. I stroke him a few more times and then lick the head of his cock like a lollipop.

"Fuck! Ah…" Eli clenches his jaw and I see the muscles in his neck strain.

I feel so powerful, commanding the strength of this beast of a man before me. I open my mouth and slowly ease as much of him into me as I can. He squeezes his eyes shut and throws his head back. I love knowing I am giving him this pleasure. Even though I just came, seeing Eli Like this has me so turned on I'm ready to go again.

"Goddamn, baby, that's it, that's so fucking it…"

When his length hits the back of my throat, I swallow him down. Eli's eyes flash open and a guttural moan rips out of him.

I continue to suck and swallow, massaging his massive length. He looks down at me with such awe and I can't wait to taste him exploding in my mouth.

Eli, however, has other plans.

He pulls out of my mouth with a pop and lifts me up into his arms.

"You're incredible, baby girl, but I want to cum inside of you. Fuck that, I *need* to cum inside of your perfect pussy."

Before I can respond, he captures my mouth in a frantic kiss, all teeth and tongue, and fire, while guiding me backward till my back hits the wall. He breaks the kiss to lift me up into his arms. My legs automatically wrap around his hips and I feel his hard cock rub up and down my slit.

"Yes," I moan, grinding against him.

He growls but continues to slide his length through my folds, not penetrating me. His cock slides across my clit, winding that coil deep within tighter and tighter with each stroke.

I feel his mouth roam over my neck, chest, nipples, and everywhere in-between. The heat of his tongue and the sting of his teeth peppering my skin and setting my nerves on fire. My fingers tangle in his hair as I hold on for dear life.

Finally, *finally,* he thrusts his cock deep inside of me while biting down on my nipple. The coil snaps and I instantly cum, pulsing and shaking in his arms. My scream is caught in my throat, I forget to breathe, all I can do is drown in wave after wave of pleasure as it washes over me and leaks out from between my thighs.

"Jesus Christ, Annaya, love when you cum on my dick, so fucking beautiful, baby, you feel so good."

Eli licks my neck and nibbles at my pulse point. I feel his lips brushing the shell of my ear. "Breathe, baby girl, take a breath for me,"

I drag air into my lungs, the oxygen pulling pleasure along with it while traveling into my bloodstream and coursing throughout my body.

I hear Eli chuckle as he pulls my earlobe through his teeth.

"Fuck, you're so sensitive. I love it. Love seeing you lost in pleasure."

All I can do is moan at this point.

"I have to move, baby."

And with that, he pulls out and slams back into me, setting a punishing pace. I feel his fingers tighten around my thighs as he holds me in place, pounding into me again and again. It hurts so fucking good, feeling his cock stretch me, his fingers bruise me, his teeth sink into me.

I tilt my head back and he covers my mouth with his, swallowing my cries in an all-consuming kiss. He rests his forehead on mine grunts with each thrust of his hips. I didn't think I had anything left in me, but I feel the pressure building again in my core, quickly overwhelming me as my legs start to shake.

What is this man doing to me?

Eli pulls his head back enough to look me in the eyes. His gaze is so intense, but I can't look away.

"Cum for me, Annaya. One more time, baby girl, I need you to cum." I close my eyes as I reach the point of no return. "Eyes on me, Annaya. I want to watch you cum."

I snap my eyes open right as pleasure overtakes my body. I feel Eli's cock swell inside of me and explode as another wave of pleasure vibrates through me, through him, through us, breathing, pulsing together as one.

"*Fuck*, Annaya, Annaya..." he chants my name over and over as the last of our orgasm slips away, dripping down between us.

The moment lasts forever. We never break eye contact, and I can see every emotion Eli is feeling, just like I know he can see all of me in this moment, so raw and unfiltered.

Eli sets me down, keeping one hand around my waist while his other hand goes behind me, bracing himself on the wall. We're both still shaking, and it seems Eli is about as unsteady as I am on my feet right now.

He tucks me into his chest, resting his forehead on the wall, covering me with his entire body, like he's shielding me from everything outside of this moment. I place a gentle kiss on his chest before burying my head there and wrapping my arms around his waist.

I wonder if he felt it too, the moment I gave him my heart, became his. The moment I gave him the power to either destroy me or make me whole.

Neither one of us says a word as we separate. Eli grabs the body wash and pours some in his hand before rubbing it all over my body, taking in every curve with such reverence. I do the same to him, soaping up his chest and arms, taking time to memorize the contours of his body.

He turns the water off and dries me with a fluffy towel, then pauses to cup my face in his hands, gently wiping away tears with his thumbs. I didn't even know I was crying.

I look into his hazel eyes and see such tenderness there, such depth. I try to look away but he turns my face back toward his.

"I felt it too, Annaya. That was..."

"Everything," I finish for him.

He nods and rests his forehead on mine.

"Don't hurt me," I whisper.

"Never, baby girl. Never."

He scoops me up in his arms and walks over to the bed, tucking me in. "You need some more sleep, sweetheart. It's been a rough week and I think I just drained you of all your energy," he says with a wink.

Eli kisses me sweetly on the forehead and then I feel him crawl in behind me and wrap me up in his arms. Eli curls around me and I feel...complete.

Chapter 11

Eli

Looking down at Annaya sleeping soundly in my arms, I finally feel complete. The stress of the last few days fades into the background and the woman lying next to me becomes my sole focus. I love her. So fucking much.

I've never experienced anything like what Annaya and I shared in the shower. God, bringing her to orgasm as soon as I sank into her was incredible. It took all my will power not to cum with her then, but I wanted it to last so much longer.

And, fuck, I'm glad I did, because when we came together...it changed everything. I already knew I loved her, but it was then that I realized I would do anything for her. She became my whole world and I saw it in her eyes too.

I saw when she surrendered herself to me, giving me every last part of her, trusting me to protect her, heal her, build her up. We both shattered in that moment. When we picked up the pieces and put each other back together, she got my heart and I got hers.

I couldn't form any words after what happened. I could barely even stand. I thought maybe it would be too much for her, but she molded herself into my chest, kissing me and nuzzling her head there like she belonged. Because she does.

When I dried her off, I saw her mind working, her eyes filling with tears. I don't think she even knew she was crying. She wasn't sad...she was confused. Like she didn't understand what it meant to be loved. I guess she probably didn't, not from what it sounded like growing up. But she will. I will show her how much I love her every damn day.

Annaya stirs in my arms and I rub slow circles on her back until she settles.

My precious girl. My strong girl. My fucking warrior who bled for her sister and defeated cancer without anyone there by her side.

It breaks my heart and enrages me at the same time to think about Annaya being all alone while kicking cancer's ass. Then she came home to parents who were too lost in their own grief to love the daughter they had left.

They still don't even see her or acknowledge her, if her dad at the fundraiser last night was any indication. He didn't even seem that concerned when I called and told him Annaya had almost been kidnapped and I was bringing her to Montana.

As much as I hate her parents, however, I will always be thankful they chose to have Annaya, even if it was for their own selfish reasons. I can't imagine my life without her. I won't ever be apart from her from this day forward. She'll never be alone again.

I pull her closer to me and breathe in her scent, letting it cover me and carry me to sleep with thoughts of her and our life together in my mind.

***

I wake up in the middle of the night to the most gorgeous woman I have ever seen kissing my chest. She has a playful look in her ocean blue eyes as she grins at me and kisses her way up toward my mouth.

How the fuck did I get so lucky?

Annaya cages me in with one arm on either side of my head and bends down to kiss me. It doesn't last nearly as long as I had hoped. Not by a long shot. I flip us over so I'm hovering over her and she's squirming beneath me.

She giggles, and it sparks something deep inside of me. I want her to always have laughter on her lips.

I can think of a few other things I want on her lips as well...

In one swift move, I gather her wrists from where she has them around my neck and raise them above her head on the bed, pinning them in place with one of my hands.

"Eli!" she shrieks with laughter. "What are you do—"

I don't wait for her to finish. I dip my head to her chest and suck her perfect breast into my mouth.

"Ohmygod..." she moans.

I kiss my way over to her other breast and give it the same attention. Leaning back slightly, I take in the sight of my beautiful Annaya stretched out before me, the moonlight casting an ethereal light over her supple skin and mouthwatering curves. I move between her thighs and dip my other hand up and down her slit to make sure she's ready for me.

"So fucking wet, Annaya," I say in approval, taking my hand from her sweet pussy and licking my fingers clean.

"Only for you, Eli."

"Shit, baby, I need you right now. Are you ready for me?"

"Please, please..." She moans and bucks her hips upward, seeking my cock.

I line myself up and slam into her. We both cry out, and Annaya's wrists strain against my hold. I feel her legs wrap around me. She digs her heels into my ass, spurring me on. I pump into her, each thrust shaking her breasts, causing my mouth to water.

Leaning down, I suck on her nipple, flicking my tongue back and forth over the sensitive pebble. I switch to the other nipple, not wanting it to feel neglected. Annaya arches her back and I reach down with my free hand to circle her clit.

"Oh, Eli, yes, yes..."

I continue pounding into her, strumming her clit, and holding her wrists. I play her body like a fucking instrument and she's making the most beautiful music. Our skin slaps together while she moans under me and I suck her tits.

It's a hard and fast fuck and it's perfect. I'm close to coming and I knew she is, too. I feel it in her muscles, the way her pussy clenches around my cock, trying to suck me in.

"Cum with me, baby girl," I growl in her ear. "Cum with me right the fuck now."

She reaches her climax and screams my name, arching her back as I feel her hot cum gush over my cock. I follow her a half-second later, roaring my release deep inside of her. I let go of her wrists and gather her in my arms while rolling over on my back.

We're a tangled mess of limbs and sweat and it's the best goddamn feeling ever.

I feel Annaya melt into my body as the last of her orgasm slips away, leaving her boneless and breathless. I kiss the top of her head and trace my fingers over her curves as she falls asleep in my arms.

I must have drifted to sleep, too, because I wake up to light streaming through the window, covering my beautiful Annaya in a blanket of sunshine. I couldn't look away from her if my life depended on it.

She must feel my gaze because she stirs from her sleep and blinks up at me with a sleepy grin on her face.

She's fucking adorable.

"Oh my God, we slept for like...thirteen hours!"

I chuckle. "I think we needed it, don't you?"

"Yeah..."

Her face darkens, remembering the last few days.

I rub small circles on her back and kiss the top of her head. "Do you want to talk about it, sweetheart?"

"Talk about what?"

"Annaya..." I lift her chin up so she's looking at me. "It's been a crazy forty eight hours. At the fundraiser—"

"Oh, shit, the fundraiser!" She sits up and runs her hands through her hair. "I have to make so many calls. I wasn't there to tear anything down, clean anything up, make sure everyone got paid, fuck, *fuck*!"

I pull her back into my chest.

"Shh, baby, the only thing you need to do is rest, it's all taken care of."

"What? How? I let everyone down, I..." Her eyes fill with tears.

"Annaya, look at me." She turns her head and I see such worry in her clear blue eyes. "You were kidnapped. Your life is in danger. You need to let work go for now. Focus on being here with me and letting me keep you safe."

"But..." she starts to protest. I cut her off with a quick kiss.

"Plus, I called the director of the board yesterday morning. I told him there was a family emergency and you would be out of town for the foreseeable future and you'd be in contact by the end of the week to make sure everything wrapped up okay. He was very understanding and sends his regards."

"You did that for me?"

I stroke her hair. How can such a simple gesture mean so much to her? It kills me that no one has ever taken care of her, and yet I love getting to fill in that role in her life.

"I thought you knew by now. I'd do anything for you, baby girl. I'd give you the whole fucking world if you asked me."

Annaya pulls me down for a slow, sweet kiss. It stretches on as she melts into me, savoring this, us. Finally, she pulls back enough to rest her forehead on mine.

"I just want you, Eli."

My heart soars in my chest.

"You have me, Annaya. All of me."

She curls up against me and I hold her, wondering how I lived so long without her.

Chapter 12

We eventually get out of bed and Eli makes us breakfast before giving me a tour of the house and the ranch.

I can't even take in all of the beauty. It's too much. Fields full of wildflowers, riding trails throughout the property, even a little pond with a weeping willow perched perfectly at the edge. It's paradise.

The barns are a little worse for wear, but this would be a perfect venue for a country wedding or a concert. It's picturesque, to say the least, and it would be an absolute dream come true to live here. Not that I'll live here. I'm sure Eli will take me back to New York once the threat has passed.

The thought of leaving here and leaving Eli causes a sharp pain in my stomach and brings tears prickling to the back of my eyes. He's my home. This feels like home, too. I never even considered a life outside of the city until now, but for some reason, I can't picture myself anywhere else.

I was running myself ragged trying to prove to my parents that I deserve love and I can make a difference even if I couldn't save my sister. But after all the shit went down at the fundraiser, and seeing my dad behave the way he did, I realized I need to live life on my own terms. I just need to figure out what, exactly, those terms are.

"What are you thinking about, sweetheart?" Eli breaks into my thoughts as we finish up the tour.

"Everything is so beautiful, Eli. It's perfect out here."

He stops walking and pulls me in for a heartbreakingly sweet kiss before resting his forehead on mine and twining our fingers together.

"It's perfect now that you're here."

I'm not sure how to interpret that. Sure, a huge part of me wants to believe he means he wants to keep me, that we could make our home here. But that small voice in my head reminds me I would be of no use here. He doesn't need me, and as much as I want to belong, I don't.

We continue our walk back to the house. I see a tall woman with graying hair pulling weeds in the garden behind the house. She's probably in her sixties, tan from long days out on the ranch.

Eli takes my hand and lifts it to his lips, kissing my knuckles.

"Ready to meet my mom?"

I stiffen as panic runs through my body.

I've never met anyone's parents before, certainly not a boyfriend's parents. Wait, is Eli my boyfriend? What even are we? And when did I become that girl who needs to define the relationship?

My own parents don't like me, I can't imagine anyone else's would either.

As if sensing my anxiety, Eli leans over and kisses my temple.

"Relax, baby. She's going to love you."

He puts his hand on the small of my back and guides me toward the house.

"Mama, I'd like you to meet Annaya. She's my..." He falters for a second and I hold my breath while he searches for the right word. I can't believe how on edge I am waiting for him to explain our relationship to his mom.

"Well, she's mine. My woman." He smiles at me and I blush.

I'm his.

The woman stands up from her position in the garden and wipes her hands on her jeans.

"Annaya, is it?" she asks with a friendly smile. I nod. "What a beautiful name! I love it. So unique and elegant. It fits you."

Why is she being so nice?

Eli rubs small circles on the small of my back, keeping me grounded.

"Thank you. It's so nice to meet you..." I never got her name, but I stick out my hand for a handshake.

"I'm Sandra, sorry my boy forgot his manners." She rolls her eyes playfully at Eli, who is grinning at her. "Can't say I blame him, pretty girl like you getting him all tongue-tied."

"Ma…" Eli says in an exasperated tone. I can almost picture him as a little kid when he says it.

"We don't shake hands around here, dearie. We hug." She pulls me in for the warmest hug and rocks me back and forth. I've never been so wholly accepted for who I am without any thought.

"You can call me mama if you want. We're family around here," she says while still hugging me.

It's too much. I can't stop the tears.

"Oh, sweet child, I didn't mean to make you cry!"

"No," I sniffle. "I'm sorry, it's not you. God, I'm a nutcase, huh?"

I try to pull away but Sandra squeezes me tighter. "If you're a nutcase, then you'll fit in perfectly here. Welcome home."

I cry some more and Sandra just holds me, much like I imagine a mom would. Well, a mom who wasn't mine.

"Okay, enough of that. I want a pie. Want to help me make one?"

I laugh and nod my head. "I have no idea how to do that, but I'd love to learn."

"Great, it's settled then." She looks over at Eli, who is pouting. "You've had her to yourself for the last month, you can share her for an afternoon."

He smiles and rolls his eyes. "Yes, Mama. She's all yours. I have some work I should get to anyway, I suppose. You go on in, I'll send Annaya in a minute."

Sandra nods and heads inside.

He takes my hand and pulls me into his chest, kissing my forehead and wiping the last of my tears. "Told you she'd love you." He smiles down at me and captures my lips in a kiss. It starts off sweet, but turns passionate, stealing the breath from my lungs. Finally, Eli pulls back and kisses my nose, cheeks, and forehead. I giggle and place one last chaste kiss on his lips. "Go have fun. I'll be back for dinner."

I turn toward the house and he swats my ass.

"Hey!" I squeal.

"Sorry, can't help myself when I'm around you," he says with a grin.

I sigh dramatically and run up to the house.

Two hours later, Sandra and I have made an apple pie and a blueberry pie. We've talked about the ranch, about her late husband, and of course, she's shared plenty of embarrassing and adorable stories about Eli growing up.

After drying off the last dish, she wipes her hands off and removes her apron. "I'm going to head back out to the garden," Sandra says, giving me a warm smile.

"I'm just going to bring some pie and coffee to Eli, then I can join you."

"Great idea, apple is his favorite. He's probably in his office – it's the first door on the right upstairs."

"Got it! Thanks again, Sandra. This was such a lovely afternoon."

She smiles and gives me a quick hug before heading outside.

I get to the office upstairs and lift my hand to knock before going inside, but I hear tense voices in the room. One is Eli's voice, and the other is an older man. It sounds like he is on speakerphone.

I don't mean to eavesdrop but I hear my dad's name.

"You messed up, kid. Presley is saying he'll only pay for the first month. As soon as you took her out of state, you breached your contract."

"What the hell was I supposed to do? Her life was in danger and my job is to protect her. The ranch is the only place I knew of that she could hide away till this all blows over," Eli says, his voice full of frustration.

I feel a sharp pain in my chest at the reminder that I'm his job and he brought me here because I needed a safe place, not because he wanted me to meet his mom and move me in.

Stupid, stupid, stupid.

I know all of these things, but I wanted so badly to believe the fantasy, that maybe he loved me as much as I love him.

"I understand why you did it, Eli. I'm just saying—"

"I know what you're saying. We're fucked. One month's pay won't cover the mortgage on this place, let alone any repairs that need to be done."

My heart sinks.

It's my fault he's not getting paid the full amount. Not only am I completely useless when it comes to helping out around the ranch, but I'm also hurting him financially.

I hate being a burden. It's an all too familiar feeling. I can't bear to hear any more, so I turn to head back downstairs, only I trip and break the plate, sending coffee and pie all over the floor.

Fuck.

Another mess that's all my fault.

I'm trying to clean up as quickly as possible and get the fuck out of here, but I hear the door open behind me. I collect the large pieces of the plate and pile them up, then start gathering the mess of pie into one big pile so it's easier to clean when I come back up with a rag.

"Annaya? What happened? Are you okay?"

"I'm sorry, I'm cleaning it up. I'll go get a rag," I try saying in a normal voice. I'm pretty sure I failed.

He kneels down in front of me, right in the puddle of coffee, not caring that his jeans will be stained. "Hey, it's okay, baby. It's not a big deal. Are you hurt?"

He grabs my wrist and turns my hand over to reveal a deep cut, blood dripping down my arm and onto the floor.

"Oh, shit, I'm sorry, I can clean it—"

He takes his shirt off and wraps it around my hand before scooping me up and carrying me to a bathroom down the hall. Eli sets me down on the edge of the tub and kneels in front of me again.

"Look at me, sweetheart. What's going on?"

I can't face him right now knowing I'm such a burden. I shake my head and repeat the only words I seem to know at the moment.

"I'm sorry. I'm sorry for everything. I'll clean it up, I'll go back to New York...I'm sorry."

"What? Why are you sorry? Look at me, Annaya." I finally let my eyes rest on his. "You didn't do anything wrong. Accidents happen. As far as going back to New York – abso-fucking-lutely not. I'm never letting you out of my sight again."

"But the money. My dad won't pay you..."

"Ah, you heard that, huh?"

"I'm sor—"

He puts his finger to my lips.

"Please stop apologizing, sweetheart, you didn't do anything wrong. It sucks about the money, but honestly, I was starting to feel weird about getting paid at all. I would make the same decision a thousand times over if I knew it would keep you safe."

"What? Why wouldn't you want to get paid?"

He looks at me for a second, like he's trying to figure me out.

"Because you're not just a job to me, Annaya. You've become my whole world."

I've wanted to hear those words from him for so long, but I can hardly believe it's happening.

"But why? I mean, why me? I'm...I'm just me."

"Baby, you're killing me. Do you really not know?"

"Know what?"

He cups my face in both of his hands and lets his gaze roam around my features – from my forehead to my nose and cheeks, over my lips, finally landing on my eyes.

"I love you, Annaya."

"You do?"

"Yes. So fucking much."

"Are you sure?"

He chuckles. "Yeah, baby girl. I'm sure."

I close my eyes as tears start to roll down my cheeks.

"Say it again."

"I love you, Annaya."

"No one has ever said that to me before."

I open my eyes and look right at Eli. Surprisingly, I see tears in his eyes.

He pulls me down into his lap and sits us on the floor, wrapping me up in his strong embrace. He nuzzles my neck and whispers, "I love you, I love you, I love you," over and over into my skin. I melt for him. My heart is so full, every part of me feels complete and whole when I'm with Eli.

I nudge his head up so he's looking at me.

"I love you too, you know."

"Are you sure?" he asks with a grin.

I smile. "Yes. One hundred percent."

I go to wrap my arms around his neck when I remember the cut. I wince as I hit my shirt- covered hand on Eli's chest.

"Oh, fuck, baby. Your hand. I totally forgot."

He gently takes my hand and unwraps the t-shirt.

Eli sets me back down on the edge of the tub and begins to clean and bandage my hand. He kisses the bandage and then leans down and crashes his lips against mine, leading us in a soul-shattering kiss, confirming our earlier sentiments of love and tenderness.

Chapter 13

The ranch is a mess, my uncle is pissed, Presley is being an annoying ass, but none of it matters because she loves me.

Annaya loves me.

I know we have a long road ahead of us to build trust and to heal from our pasts but hearing Annaya say those words was the best fucking thing that has ever happened to me.

After I bandaged her up, she insisted she go back outside and help my mom in the garden, despite my protests about her hand. She promised to take it easy, and honestly, I didn't have the heart to keep her from my mom.

It makes me so happy to see them together, especially knowing Annaya has never had a family like that. I love providing that for her. I know she's going to make a great mom one day. Hopefully soon.

Yeah, I'm all in. All fucking it. I want it all with her.

While Annaya has been out in the garden, I've been squaring things away with her father. I told him Annaya would be my responsibility from here on out. He was confused at first and reiterated he wouldn't be paying me. I assured him I don't want his money, I only want Annaya.

Finally, he's starting to understand.

"So you've been fucking my daughter, eh?"

"I love her, Mr. Moretti."

"Annaya?" he asks as if he's genuinely confused.

What is this guy's fucking problem?

"Presley. Now that I am no longer employed by you, I feel that I can speak freely. Annaya is the most amazing person I have ever met. I don't know what she sees in me, but I'm the luckiest bastard on the face of the earth that she would even consider being mine. I know you lost a daughter, and I know that you blame Annaya for that loss."

"Eli…" he growls.

"No more," I plow on ahead, needing to get this off my chest. "She has been wanting your love and attention for so long and you have denied her at every turn. So let me make this clear. It is your absolute loss that you were too blind by your grief to see the brilliant, strong, stunning woman Annaya has turned out to be, no thanks to you. She is mine. I am hers. I will be taking care of her from now on. Do you understand?"

"Boy, don't you—"

"*Do. You. Understand?*" I say again with more force.

There's silence on the line for a minute and then I finally hear, "Yes."

Then Presley hangs up.

Good riddance.

I head downstairs to dinner, already missing Annaya even though we've only been apart for a few hours. When I get to the dining room, I can tell Mom and Annaya have been planning something. They look awfully suspicious.

"Good evening, ladies," I say as I give my mother a kiss on the cheek before sitting down next to Annaya and pulling her in for a proper kiss.

"Eli!" she squeals. "Not in front of your *mom*," she whispers that last part.

"Oh, dearie, I'm old, not dead. I'm glad to see my son so happy. Maybe I'll be a grandma soon?" She winks and Annaya blushes a deep red.

I kiss her forehead and wrap an arm around her waist, holding her close to my side.

"Okay, out with it, you two," I say.

My mom is feigning innocence, not well, might I add, and Annaya gets a huge grin on her face.

"So… I was thinking…" she starts. I smile and rub small circles with the hand I have at her hip to encourage her to continue. "I know the ranch needs some repairs, and I know how much you both love it here, and God, I love it too. I mean what's not to love?"

She looks at me and I want to kiss her again, but I also want to know what she's been thinking and planning.

"Anyway, I think with a few basic repairs, we could have a decent venue. We could put on a spring party with barbecue, live music, and horse rides. We could provide blankets and have people dine picnic-style by the pond, maybe set up some face painting for the kids, a few fun little carnival games..."

I'm completely blown away. She wants to help save the ranch? Could that possibly mean she wants to stay? I don't even know how to express what all of this means to me.

"I was talking with your mom, and she thought it sounded like a good idea. We could charge admission, extra for horse rides, and also advertise the empty stalls you guys have that can be rented out. If things work out, we could use the space for weddings, maybe make the spring party an annual thing, add a fall party too..."

This has to mean she wants to stay. She's talking about annual events, which means she'd have to be here year after year to put it on, right? I realize Annaya is staring up at me, waiting for a response. I haven't said anything since she started talking.

"Annaya, I..."

"I'll do everything," she blurts out. "I want to, and your mom wants to help. You won't have to worry about anything. I think if I get started tomorrow we can—"

I cut her off with a kiss, pouring out all of the gratitude and admiration I have for her. I pull back and kiss her nose and forehead.

"Annaya, that sounds like a brilliant plan. I can't believe you want to help out around here. Thank you."

"Well, yeah. Of course. I'm barging in on your home and your family and your business and I just saw a way I could pitch in. I don't know anything about horses or breeding or... Honestly, I have no idea what exactly you do on a ranch, but I can do this one thing. It'll give me something to do while I'm here for the next..."

She trails off because we haven't talked about any of it yet, the threat, the trial, her dad. Not that any of it matters. She's staying with me. She's mine.

"How about forever?" my mom chimes in, clearly on the same wavelength as me.

"Ma..."

She holds her hands up in surrender. "I'll go check on dinner." She winks at me and then mouths, *"don't fuck this up."*

I don't plan to.

Annaya is looking down at her lap. I hold her chin gently between my thumb and forefinger and lift her head up to look at me.

"Annaya, I want you here, by my side. You aren't barging in, and to be clear, you do *not* owe us anything. I never want you to feel like you are only worth what you can provide. Never again, love." She tries to look away again, but I cup her cheek and guide her face back to mine. "That being said, I know you love your job, and I know you're damn good at it. I'm so grateful you want to help out. I never would have thought of something like this. You're perfect."

I graze my thumb over her lips and caress her cheek with feather-light touches.

Her brow knits together and her eyes search mine like she's trying to peer deep down into my very soul and see if I'm telling her the truth. She wants to believe me, to trust me, but I can tell she doesn't know how. I lift her out of her chair and onto my lap so she's straddling me, and I wrap her up in my arms, tucking her head into my chest.

"I love you so much, baby girl. I meant every word I said."

"I love you too, Eli. Thank you."

"For what?"

"For giving me...a *home,*" she whispers.

I squeeze her tight and then lift her head to seal her lips with mine. She digs her fingers into my hair and pulls me closer while grinding down on my aching cock.

I force myself to cut the kiss short, seeing as we still have to eat dinner with my mom, and I'm already sporting a painful erection. Annaya pouts and I bite her bottom lip before licking away the sting.

"Later, love. I promise."

She smiles and climbs off me, giving me a knowing grin as she eyes my hard dick.

"I'll go see if your mom needs help."

I nod and watch her sashay her little ass into the kitchen. God, this woman. I love her so fucking much.

Chapter 14

Annaya

Eli, Sandra, and I had a lovely dinner followed by pie for dessert. We decided to end the evening on the porch, Eli with a beer and Sandra and I with a glass of wine.

I can honestly say this has been the best day of my life. I feel so full of love – and pie. Eli makes me feel safe, wanted, and needed, but not in a way that makes me feel used like my parents did with Alysa.

Throughout the whole evening, Eli has found little ways to touch me. A hand on my knee at dinner, resting his hand on the small of my back as he guides me outside, brushing my hair behind my ear, kissing my temple, lacing his fingers in mine. He makes me feel so cherished.

As the evening drags on, his touches become a little more heated. A hand on the knee turns into a hand on my upper thigh, massaging me lightly. A hand on the small of my back turns into a hand squeezing my ass. Brushing my hair behind my ear turns into fingers ghosting along the side of my neck.

It's been going on for hours now as we sit on the porch, and I'm wound so tight I swear to God I might cum from him just kissing me.

I've loved watching the sunset with Sandra and chatting her up about the history of the ranch, but now I'd like for her to go to bed and take her hearing aids out so I can fuck her son till our bones melt.

Eli must be thinking the same thing. Sandra is on the porch swing dozing off while Eli and I share the love seat. He pulled me onto his lap a while ago and wrapped a blanket around us. I'm sitting with my back to his front, leaning into his chest.

I feel his hand travel from its relatively innocent spot on my hip, across my tummy, and down to cup my mound over my yoga pants. My thighs instinctively squeeze together and I hear Eli's soft chuckle as he dips his head to my shoulder and places a soft kiss there.

"All I can think about is bending you over that porch railing and taking you from behind," he whispers into my shoulder.

Good thing the wind is blowing and the crickets and frogs are all out in full swing tonight. Otherwise, his mom might have gotten an earful of her son's dirty mouth.

I grind down on his half-hard cock and position my hand to stroke him through his jeans. He coughs back a groan as my fingers graze him, and I feel him lengthen and harden at my touch.

Eli presses his fingers down on my pussy, rubbing me through the thin material. I move my hips into his touch, rubbing my ass over his cock again and again. Eli can't hold back his groan this time.

Sandra snores once, loudly, then stirs awake.

We both sit still and Eli casually asks me what I have to get done tomorrow to get started on the spring party.

"Oh goodness. I must have fallen asleep for a little bit. I guess I better head inside."

She gets up and collects her wine glass and blanket.

"Have a good night, mom."

"You too. Goodnight, Annaya."

"Night, Sandra."

She takes her sweet time walking to the door and I can tell Eli is just as eager for her to leave as I am. Finally, she opens the door and we hear her walk upstairs.

Eli rips the blanket off us and stands up with me in his arms. He spins me around and attacks my lips, biting, sucking, devouring me as his hands grab my ass and press me against him.

I instinctively wrap my arms around his neck and wrap a leg around his hip. Eli catches my leg, holding it against him. I rub my soaking pussy over his hard cock and we both moan at the contact.

"I need to fuck you, baby girl. Need it like my next breath."

I nod and he sets my leg down, walking me backward till my back hits the porch railing. He kneels in front of me and hooks his thumbs inside my yoga pants and panties, pulling them down.

Eli follows the material down my right leg with his mouth, kissing every inch of skin that is revealed. He helps me step out of my pants and resumes kissing me up my left leg. Eli stops to place a kiss on my pussy, and then stands up to take my mouth in his, chasing my tongue and sucking it into his mouth.

He breaks the kiss and trails his lips down my jaw, licking and nipping at my neck. I feel his hands on my hips as he spins me around, so my back is to his front.

Eli's rough hand slides under my shirt and pulls the cup of my bra down so he can tease my breast. His other hand snakes lower, his fingers teasing me and rubbing my swollen bundle of nerves. Then he pinches my clit and sinks his teeth into my shoulder. I have to put my hand over my mouth to keep me from crying out.

Eli chuckles.

"It's okay, no one can hear us. Mom's deaf without her hearing aids and we're the only house around for miles. Scream for me, Annaya. I want to hear you fall apart." He bites my earlobe and I reach back to spear my fingers through his hair.

He continues to rub my clit in long, lazy strokes. I jerk my hips every time he bumps my hard nub.

"I love how wet you are for me, love feeling your sweet honey dripping all over my fingers," Eli murmura right before thrusting two fingers inside of me.

"Oh my *God...*" I moan.

"That's it, baby."

His fingers pump in and out of me and his other hand goes to my hip, holding me in place while he thrusts his jean covered cock up against my ass. I'm so close, right there, one more swipe over my clit and I know I'm going to explode, but then he stops.

I whine in protest. Eli chuckles and I hear him undo his jeans and pull them down. His silky, thick cock brushes back and forth between my folds, rubbing my clit and teasing my entrance.

"Fuck me, please, Eli. Please, I need you."

"Hands on the railing, love. Bend over and show me that gorgeous ass of yours."

I do as he says, bending over the railing and holding myself steady with my hands. He runs his fingers up and down my spine and then I feel the sharp crack of his palm on my ass.

I cry in surprise, but then my pussy gushes and I moan.

"Fuck, do you like that? Like when I spank you?"

"Mmm...more..." I gasp. I had no idea I liked spanking, but fuck. I do. I really do.

He spanks my other cheek and I cry out. One more hard crack of his palm, and then Eli shoves his cock into my pussy, bottoming out in one powerful thrust. It stretches me in the best way possible and I throw my head back as a feral moan escapes my mouth, pushing my ass against him.

"Goddamnit, baby girl. Fuck. You feel so good, I can't get enough of you."

He pulls out and slams into me again. Again. Again. His fingers grip my hips hard enough to bruise. I can't wait to wear his marks like a badge of honor. Eli's hands slide up my body and over my shoulders until they are gripping the rail on either side of my hands. His entire body is draped over me. I feel his muscles flex and tighten on my ass and back as he pistons himself in and out of me.

"Eli, I-I'm..."

His lips brush over my neck before I feel him sucking on my skin. "Me too, baby," he growls. "Cum with me. I've got you. Cum for me, Annaya."

I'm so there, so close. Eli reaches down and furiously rubs my clit. Sweat covers my body in a thin sheen. My breaths are shallow and my body tenses and prepares for the wave of sensations waiting on the other side of the cliff.

"I won't cum without you, so please, fucking cum, baby, I want to feel that pussy pop... *Fuck*!" He explodes inside of me as my cunt snaps around his cock, the feeling so intense I'm barely aware of the scream ripping from my throat.

Or maybe it's Eli's scream.

We both make primal noises as Eli ruts into me, hard and deep, releasing rope after rope of cum. Our combined juices make a mess down my thighs. My legs give out and I feel Eli's arm wrap around my hips, keeping me in place while he thrusts into me two more times.

We shudder and shake together, slowly regaining control of our breathing.

"Goddamn, Annaya." He kisses between my shoulder blades before resting his head there.

"Yeah." I agree and then laugh. "Every time with you is amazing."

I feel him nod against my back and then kiss me one last time. We both groan when he pulls out of me. Eli tucks himself away and helps me put my pants back on. Then, he scoops me up and throws me over his shoulder.

I shriek and then laugh when he swats my ass and carries me inside to the shower.

Twenty minutes later, we're climbing into bed naked. Eli spoons around me, holding me close. I love feeling his skin on my skin.

"I love you, Eli. Love when you touch me, kiss me, hold me. Love you so much."

He pulls me even closer to his chest. "I love you, baby girl. More than you know."

Eli kisses the top of my head and nuzzles his face there. We drift off to sleep and I'm the happiest I've ever been.

I wake up in the pitch-black room when I feel Eli's fingers rubbing my pussy. I push back against him and he groans into my neck before placing kisses up my shoulder and nibbling on my pulse point.

"Sorry to wake you, love. I have an ache only you can fix."

His hand traces over my hip and lifts my top leg over his. I feel his rock-hard cock slide into my entrance. Everything is so much more intense in the dark, my other senses heightened. Eli hisses as he pushes himself further into me, so slowly.

I moan when I feel him hit my womb, and then he starts pulling out slowly. He keeps up the excruciatingly slow pace, building us up one stroke at a time. I press back against him when he pushes in, and I squeeze around him when he pulls out, creating the most exquisite friction.

His hand spreads out over my lower belly, keeping me pressed close against him and tightening that pressure already gathering at my core.

Eli rests his head on my shoulder. I can feel his tense muscles as he controls his movements, commanding both of our bodies with his steady rhythm. It's a slow burn, but I feel the fire catching, licking at my nerves, sending a rush of heat between my legs.

"That's it, fuck, baby, love being inside of you, love how wet you get for me." He picks up his pace slightly and my muscles spasm with each thrust. "So goddamn tight. You feel incredible, love. Are you there, baby? I need you to cum for me. Cum on my big cock."

He thrusts once, twice, three times and I convulse in his arms, squirting all over him and trembling from my orgasm.

"Jesus, you made a mess, baby girl. I fucking love it." He pounds into me, rubbing my clit with his fingers, one orgasm tumbling into another as he fucks into me, pushing me higher and higher.

"Annaya, fuck, Annaya..." he chants over and over, his cock swelling and exploding inside of me. The force of his release triggers a final, deep orgasm to break out over my body.

I curl in on myself, so sensitive from all of my orgasms. Eli just holds me in his arms, thrusting lazily as we both come down.

"I've got you, baby, I've got you," he whispers as he nuzzles his head into my hair. "Thank you, love.

We fall asleep like that, with Eli still inside of me.

Chapter 15

I wake up still spooned around Annaya. My dick fell out of her at some point during the night, much to my dismay. I would love nothing more than to be inside her twenty-four-seven.

Watching my beautiful girl sleep, I take time to admire her perfect body. My fingers trace along the curve of her hip, down the dip of her waist, and up her ribcage, all the way to her shoulder. I work my way back down and then repeat my path. She's so fucking gorgeous. Flawless. Mine.

Annaya stirs and turns to face me. I'm hit again with those piercing blue eyes.

"Morning, handsome," she says, smiling up at me.

"Morning, beautiful," I reply, tucking some loose hair behind her ear.

I lean down to kiss her, but she covers her mouth. I frown at her and she giggles.

"I have morning breath, Eli. You can't kiss me!"

"I don't give a fuck about morning breath. I need your lips on mine. Right now, woman!"

She lets me take her mouth in mine and lead us in a slow kiss. She's crazy because all I taste is her sweetness.

"You're so bossy," she says once we break apart.

"You like it," I whisper as I nuzzle her neck and caress her back. My hand lands on her ass and I pull her into me, relishing the feel of her skin, her heat, her smell.

"Oh, no, mister." Annaya places her small hands on my chest and pushes me back a little. "I need to get to work. And I don't need your distractions."

I grin at her. "Are you sure?" I ask before dipping my head down and latching on to one of her breasts. I lick her nipple until it's a hard peak and then I bite down on it.

"Oh, God, Eli..."

I reach down and run my finger through her wetness, teasing her entrance. She winces, and I pull my hand out from between her thighs, feeling like an asshole.

"Are you sore, sweetheart?"

"Maybe a little." She looks down, not meeting my gaze. "Sorry," she whispers.

I lift her chin up, our faces inches apart.

"There's nothing to apologize for, Annaya. It's my fault for being rough with you. I never want to cause you pain."

She smiles devilishly at me. "But it felt so good."

I groan. "You're not making it easy for me to let you out of this bed, baby."

I kiss her again, unable to help myself.

Eventually, I pull back and kiss her forehead. "Now get your sexy ass up and dressed before I lose control."

"What if I like it when you lose control?" she asks as she wiggles down the bed and stands up. I growl and smack her ass as she walks by. "Eli!" she giggles.

I lift my hands up in surrender and grin at her. Annaya rolls her eyes but grins right back. I reluctantly watch her dress and get ready for the day before finally pulling some clothes on myself.

Five hours later, it's early afternoon and I've been plugging away in my office all day. Annaya has stopped in a few times to get my approval on some things for the spring party, but I trust whatever she wants to do. I can't say I don't mind seeing her though, so I let her come to me for whatever details she wants to discuss.

I hear a light knock at the door before my mom comes in.

"What's up?" I ask. She sits down on the couch in the corner of the office and motions for me to come join her. "Uh-oh. Is this going to be a serious talk?"

"Oh shut up and get over here."

I have to laugh at my feisty mom. Sitting down next to her, I turn toward the second most important woman in my life. She takes my large hand in her smaller, more fragile one.

"Eli, I'm so happy you found Annaya."

"Me too, ma. She's the most amazing woman I've ever met, even if I didn't want to admit it at first."

"Well, I see why you love her, son. I love her, too. She doesn't come from a very loving family, does she?"

I shake my head. Her story isn't mine to tell, so I don't go into all of the details. "No, she's been without anyone to love her for most of her life."

"She has us now." Mom squeezes my hand again.

"Are we just talking about how much we love Annaya? I mean, I'm all for that, but you seem like there's something else you want to tell me."

"There is." She takes a deep breath and fiddles with her wedding ring. "I don't want to meddle, and I don't want to pressure you, but I do want you to have this."

She takes the ring off her finger and places it in the palm of my hand.

"Ma..."

"It was your great grandmother's ring on your father's side. It was always meant to go to you."

"Mom... are you sure about this?" I lift the ring up.

"Absolutely. I've seen you two together. She looks at you like you hung the moon, and I know you cherish her with everything you have inside. You are very lucky to have found a love like that, son."

We hug and I hear her sniffle a little bit.

She pulls back and swats me playfully on the chest. "Now you go put that ring on her finger so I can have me some grandbabies!"

I laugh and nod my head as she makes her way out of the office.

Chapter 16

Annaya

It's been almost three weeks since I came to stay with Eli and his mom. I've loved every single second.

When I'm not helping out Sandra in the kitchen or planning the spring party, I'm with Eli. We spend our time exploring the property as well as the charming little town. Every night we fall into bed, chasing our pleasure and finding release together.

I know we've talked about this place being my home too, but I still can't fully wrap my head around it. We haven't talked about the trial or the bounty on my head. There are a lot of unanswered questions but I'm just trying to enjoy my little slice of paradise while I have it.

It's not just Eli and his mom I've grown attached to, it's the whole goddamn town. Planning this spring party has been so fun and everyone I talk to is just as excited, if not more so than I am.

Most of the events I planned in New York were so high pressure. I thought I enjoyed the stress and adrenaline rush that comes with high stakes. But that's because I didn't know it could be like this.

I'm not even sure what *this* is. It's slower than New York for sure, and I'm not going toe to toe with vendors trying to get the best price. I feel like I'm a part of something bigger – a community of people who truly want to help. I've gotten so many donations and people are coming up and asking me how they can help, thanks to the word of mouth around town.

The spring party is tomorrow, and I can't wait for Eli to see everything. I've kept him out of the main barn and field where we're hosting the band and serving the food.

I can tell he's been a little preoccupied these last few days and I don't want to stress him out or put anything else on his plate. He has a lot riding on this—literally his livelihood—and I feel so honored that he's trusting me.

It's almost time for dinner, and Sandra and I have been cooking up a storm. I'm so thankful she's been willing to teach me how to prepare food. It's nice to have the ability to make something for myself other than smoothies and take-out.

Eli pops his head into the kitchen, giving me a soft smile. "Annaya, can I steal you for a minute?"

I follow him to the office and wonder what he wants to talk about.

Once the door is closed, he pushes me against it and kisses me, pulling my hips into his.

"I've been wanting to do that for the last three hours, but I couldn't pry you away from my mom."

"Jealous?" I tease.

"Maybe," He whispers before trailing kisses down my neck and nibbling at my shoulder.

"Well then *maybe* I can make it up to you." I grin up at him while my hand travels down his chest and over his abs, resting on his belt buckle.

I feel Eli's hand grasp my wrist lightly and pull my hand away.

"You have no idea how much I want that, baby girl, but I actually have some things to discuss with you." I pout and he chuckles, placing a chaste kiss on my lips. "It's about your dad."

My mood instantly changes.

"Oh."

Eli guides me to the couch, and we sit down.

"The trial is over. The thugs were convicted and with them, a huge portion of the underground crime scene in New York was outed. Those cases will take years to process and come to a close, but the point is, you're safe now. There's no bounty on your head and everyone else involved is keeping their heads down and crawling back into the shadows."

"Oh," I say again.

Now that I don't have to be here, will he still want me? I know he loves me, but was he just saying that so I wouldn't feel bad about staying with him?

Then again, he can't fake when we're together. Every time with Eli is incredible, and I can feel him showing me with his body how much he loves me. Still, I can't shake this feeling there's something he's been keeping from me.

"This is good news, sweetheart."

"Yeah, I know." I try to smile at him, but he furrows his brow.

I suddenly remember the first thing I did when planning for the spring party. Looking back, I see that it may have been incredibly stupid. I don't regret it, but it might make my life complicated when I get back to New York.

That's okay. Eli won't ever find out anyway.

"What's wrong, love?"

"Nothing. It's just a lot to take in." It's not a lie, it's just not what he thinks. "You said there were things, plural, to discuss. What else is going on?"

"Well, I was going over the books for this last month and I noticed none of the checks I gave you for the spring party were cashed."

Oh, shit. I guess he might find out after all.

"Well, you know a lot of things have been donated, so the overall cost is much lower than I initially estimated."

"Right, but surely there were *some* overhead costs. I remember approving construction plans for the barn, not to mention the permits, and the extra help we hired to clean up the stables and grounds."

I pick at an imaginary piece of lint on my jeans, hoping to stall and come up with an answer.

"I'm not mad, I'm just confused, sweetheart. How are we paying for this if my checks weren't cashed? I'm not worried about the money. I know we're going to make it all back and then some, I have absolute confidence in you. Just tell me what's going on."

I look up at him and take a deep breath.

"I sold my apartment to pay for the party," I blurt out all at once.

Eli's eyebrows shoot up to his hairline and his jaw literally drops. It'd be funny if I weren't so nervous about telling him everything. He doesn't say anything, so I plow ahead, wanting to get the next part out as fast as possible.

"I can't explain it, exactly. Something happened when I woke up here that first day. I felt safe and warm even though my life was in danger. Then there was that moment in the shower where my whole world changed. And I then met your mom and we baked apple pies and...and...shit, I know it was stupid, but I just felt like I belonged here. I was high off of you telling me you loved me, and so..."

I wipe my hands down my jeans and then ball them into fists before continuing.

"I listed my apartment and of course it sold within a week. I'm just...I'm so thankful for you and your mom and this town and I want this to be perfect. I want you to get as much money as you can out of this event. It was short-sighted of me, though. I'm sure I can find a cheaper place when I get back. I mean who needs to live on Park Avenue, right?"

I laugh and wave my hand in the air to show how ridiculous and high maintenance that whole lifestyle is.

Eli still hasn't said anything. He's just staring at me. I can't figure out the look on his face. So I just keep blabbing because I can't stand the silence stretching between us. I stand up and pace in front of him.

"But, anyway, you just said the threat is over, which reminded me that I'm only here temporarily, which is fine." *And by "fine" I mean it will be pure torture to walk away.* "I just got caught up in the fantasy of being here, you know? But after the spring party tomorrow I can look at flights back—"

"No!" Eli booms, finally finding his voice. I jump at his sharp tone and the tears that I've held back flood my eyes and spill over my cheeks.

"I'm sorry, Eli, I just wanted to help," I choke on a sob. I hate that I've disappointed him, and I feel like such a fucking idiot.

He rushes over to me, cupping my face in his hands. "Don't cry, love, please don't cry." He wipes my tears away with his thumbs, his voice much gentler now. "I'm sorry I yelled, I...this is a lot for me to process. When I heard you say you were leaving after tomorrow, I snapped. You're not fucking leaving me. But we can discuss that later."

He takes a deep breath, gathering his thoughts. He lowers his hands to my hips, gripping them tightly like I might run away from him at any second.

"First things first. You sold your apartment?"

I nod.

"To pay for the spring party?"

I nod again.

"Because you want to stay here with me?"

I shrug and stare down at my feet. Eli tilts my head up with his forefinger.

"Look at me, sweetheart."

"Yes. I want to stay here. With you."

Eli leans in and presses his lips to mine, urgently seeking entrance. I open up and he sweeps his tongue inside, swirling around mine in a hungry, desperate way like he wants to consume me. When he breaks the kiss, we're both panting for air.

He leans his forehead against mine.

Then he sinks down on one knee.

What the hell is he doing?

"I want that too, baby girl. I want you here with me. Forever." He reaches into his pocket and pulls out a ring. "I was going to do this tomorrow at the spring party, but, fuck, I need you to know how serious I am about you, Annaya. I love you. Love you like I've never loved anyone.

"Eli..."

"Let me get this out," he says with a nervous smile. "You own me, love. I didn't have all of the details planned out yet, but you sold your apartment." He pauses, the look in his eyes one of wonder. "You sold your fucking apartment for me, for us. Baby, that's huge. I don't even know how to begin to thank. Not just for this event, but for everything. Saving me. Healing me. I don't know how I made it this long without you, but now that I have you, I can't let you go. Not ever."

I still can't believe what's happening.

"Annaya will you marry me?"

Looking down at Eli, his hazel eyes pleading with me to be his wife, I finally register what he's saying. He wants me. *Me.* Forever.

"Yes!" I half sob, half cry out with joy.

His face practically splits in half with his gigantic smile as relief washes over his eyes.

"Are you sure?" he asks with a grin.

I kneel down in front of him, both of us on our knees now, and pepper his face with kisses. "Yes, yes, yes," I say in between kisses.

He takes my left hand and places the ring on it.

"Wait, is this your mom's ring?" I loved her ring when I saw it. It looked antique with a stunning pear-shaped diamond and an intricate band laced with smaller diamonds on the edges.

"It was my great-grandma's ring. My mom gave it to me a few days after you came here to stay with us. She knew you were the one just like I did."

I can't handle the emotions swirling around inside of me. It's too much. Too perfect.

"Do you like it?" He asks, looking worried at my tears.

"Eli, it's perfect. I can't take it though. It's your family's ring."

"*You*, Annaya, are my family. I want you to have this ring. I want you to be my wife, have my children, grow old with me. I want forever, and I want it with you."

I hug him and cry into his shoulder.

"Tell me what you're thinking, love." He strokes my back and turns his head to kiss my temple.

"I just never thought I'd have a family heirloom. I...I never thought I'd have a family."

Eli leans back and sits on his heels, pulling me onto his lap so I'm straddling him. He takes my left hand and kisses my ring before placing my hand over his heart and covering it with his. I feel his other hand at the nape of my neck, pulling me closer so he can rest his forehead on mine.

"I'm your family, baby girl. Always."

I nod against his forehead. "Mine," I whisper.

"Mine," he repeats.

Epilogue

Eli

Three Months Later...

Of course, the spring party was a huge success.

I have no idea how Annaya did it all. The ranch never looked so good. She somehow transformed the old barn into a rustic and chic environment with a chandelier and some well-placed lighting.

She renovated the inside and went above and beyond what I thought she was going to do. We were able to not only save the ranch, but buy new horses to breed, hire three new ranch hands, and still have money in the bank.

Ma was ecstatic, and not just about the success of the spring party. She bawled as soon as she saw the ring on Annaya's finger.

She insisted on looking for a new place to live, but Annaya wouldn't have it. We compromised by using some of the spring party profits to build Mom a house on the property. That way she would be close, but we'd still have our privacy.

Which is a good thing, because I can't get enough of Annaya. I've fucked her in every room of the house, on every available surface. I can't decide which one is my favorite.

I love sinking into her while she's spread out on the kitchen table, but I also love when she rides me on the couch, and when I take her from behind while she's leaning over my desk. Fuck. Just thinking about it gets me hard.

She's been extra horny lately, which is saying something. Lately, she's been finding me in the middle of the day, sneaking into the barn so I can take her up against the wall, or pulling me into the nearest room in the house so she can suck me off before I bury my head between her thighs.

Yesterday we went on a walk around the pond and she shoved me up against the weeping willow and begged me to fuck her out in the open. I couldn't say no to her. Not that I wanted to.

Our wedding is in a week and I cannot wait to make her my wife. She's planned every detail, of course, but I wanted to be involved in the process as well.

I've loved getting to see a little bit into her process of planning things, and as always, I'm amazed at her talent. We're having the wedding here, of course. She wants to get married by the pond, under the weeping willow. I will be thinking dirty thoughts of our tryst together the entire time, I'm sure of it.

Annaya has drummed up business around town for planning events and parties. It's on a much smaller scale than in New York, but I think she likes the slower pace and the community she's building into.

There's a knock on my office door, pulling me out of my thoughts.

My beautiful bride to be pokes her head in and gives me a radiant smile when her eyes meet mine. I swear she's glowing.

God, this woman undoes me in ways I can't even begin to understand.

"Hey, love, what's up?" I ask. I stand up and walk over toward her, unable to keep my distance any longer. Whenever she's around I have to have my hand on her, be near her in some way.

"I, uh, I have something to tell you." Her brow furrows and she stares at her feet. I can't stand to see her like this.

I cup her face and gently guide her up to meet my gaze.

"What is it, love? You can tell me anything."

"I don't know how this happened. I mean, I *know* how it happened..." Tears well up in her eyes and she looks tentative, scared, almost. I wrap her up in my arms. I don't know how she went from her brilliant shining self to crying in a matter of minutes, but I'm determined to fix it.

"What happened? What's wrong?"

She pulls away from me and I reluctantly let her, though I keep my hands on her hips.

"Eli, I'm pregnant."

My world turns upside down.

Pregnant.

I can't fucking believe it. I'm going to be a dad. She's going to be the mother of my children. It's everything I've been dreaming about for weeks. If I'm honest, it's everything I've been dreaming about since I first met her.

So many emotions rush through me, overwhelming joy being at the top of the list. I look in her eyes and she seems unsteady like she's bracing herself for my reaction. Does she think I'm mad?

I kneel before her and kiss her belly, thinking of my kid growing inside of her at this very moment.

"Thank you, thank you, Annaya." I look up at her beautiful face and she gives me a confused look. "Sweetheart, I'm so goddamn happy. I want you to have all my babies." I smile up at her, hoping to ease some of her worry.

"You do?" she squeaks out.

"Hell yes."

"Are you sure?" She goes for our little inside joke, but I hear it laced with a bit of doubt still.

I stand up and kiss away her tears, wrapping one arm around her waist to pull her closer while the other one goes to the nape of her neck to hold her in place while I move my mouth from her cheeks to her lips, claiming her and showing her just how much I want her.

I feel her wrap her arms around my waist and melt into me. I break the kiss to look at this perfect woman in my arms. She buries her head into my chest and I kiss the top of her head before resting my forehead there.

"I love you. I love our baby. I can't wait to be your husband, to be the father of our kid."

"What if I'm a terrible mother? I didn't exactly have a great example growing up."

I pull back slightly and lift her chin so we're face to face.

"Annaya, listen to me. You will be the best mother. You may not have had great parents, but you know how to love. You know what it was like growing up without affection, so I know you will lavish it all the more on our child. I have no doubts. You will be an amazing mother, and I can't wait to meet our kid."

She kisses me sweetly and buries her face in my shoulder. I rest my head on hers again, rubbing comforting circles on her back.

"You're growing my baby inside of you," I exclaim, almost yelling, still completely blown away by the news.

"Yup," she says and laughs a little into my shirt.

"How are you feeling? Do you have morning sickness? Do we need to go to the doctor? Do you need to sit down? Can I get you anything?"

A flood of questions washes over me and pours right out of my mouth. I was protective and attentive to Annaya before the pregnancy, and now it seems those tendencies have gone into overdrive.

She leans back and smiles. "I'm okay, I promise. I feel fine." Annaya peers up at me with so much love in her eyes. "You're really happy? You really want a family with me?"

I tuck a few strands of loose hair behind her ear and rest my forehead on hers.

"I already told you, baby girl, you *are* my family. Forever. I can't wait to share our love with this little one." I take a step back and kneel in front of her again, kissing her belly and resting my head on it.

She tangles her fingers in my hair and pushes me down ever so slightly.

I look up and grin at her, raising an eyebrow.

"Do you need something from me, love?"

"Yes," she breathes out. "I ache for you. All the time."

I groan and ease her back into the wall. Lifting her dress up, I see she's not wearing any panties.

I lift one of her legs over my shoulder to give me better access. I flatten my tongue and lick her from her entrance to her clit, circling her sensitive bundle of nerves.

"God, Eli."

She rocks her hips into me, urging me on. I spear my tongue deep inside of her, tasting her honey straight from the source. Massaging her walls with my tongue, I reach out and begin rubbing her clit, winding her up till her muscles quiver with tension, bracing for sweet release.

Then I pull back, leaving her on the edge.

"Noooo!" she protests.

"You know I'll always take care of you, love."

I strip my clothes off in record time and lift her by her ass, pressing her into the wall while her legs go around my hips.

"Please, please let me cum, I need to, need it so bad..."

I bend down and lick the slender column of her neck, nibbling just below her ear like I know she loves. I rock into her, sliding my thick, angry cock up and down her soaking wet slit, not pushing into her just yet.

Her legs shake as I push her toward the edge again, feeling her entire body go rigid in my arms. Again, I pull back.

Annaya practically screams in frustration, but then I slam my aching cock into her in one thrust and her cries turn into moans as she falls apart in my arms. I swallow her sounds as I kiss her, feeling her tight pussy pulse around my hard length. Her orgasm holds her body hostage as she writhes against the wall, rubbing herself on my dick, riding out her ecstasy.

When she relaxes into my body, I tighten my grip on her ass and slowly slide out of her only to pound back inside her warmth. The sounds we make are obscene, her juices leaking out all over my cock, dripping down her legs. I look down and see her pussy swallow me, still pulsing from her orgasm.

"Fuck, baby, look at us, look at how we fit together. It's fucking perfect."

God, I could watch this all day, watch her tight, hot cunt stretch over me.

Annaya rolls her hips and digs her fingernails into my shoulders, clearly getting as much satisfaction from watching us as I am.

"Shit, Eli, I'm so close...I...don't stop..."

I rest my forehead on hers, sweat dripping down my face as I rut into her like a fucking animal.

"Yes, yes, yes..."

She cums again, sinking her teeth into my shoulder. Her whole body squeezes around mine as her pussy sucks me in. Annaya claws at my back, trying to get closer to me, trying to fuse her being with mine.

"Jesus Christ, Annaya. So goddamn good, so good, baby girl."

I thrust into her two more times before erupting deep inside of her.

My legs start shaking and I carefully guide us to the floor, a tangled heap of limbs. I roll on my back and pull Annaya with me, tucking her into my side.

"Are you okay, baby? I wasn't gentle. I'll have to be more careful with you now."

"Don't you dare!" She looks up at me with furrowed brows. "I'm perfect. I feel perfect. Like...like I'm home."

I pull her closer, kissing her forehead.

"You are, love. You're home."

Annaya curls up on my chest and sighs so sweetly. This woman. I can't imagine my life without her. Good thing I don't have to.

Also by Cameron Hart

Check out my other popular series and books!
Mafia, MC, & Bodyguard Romance:
<u>Moscatelli Crime Family Series</u>[1]
<u>Di Salvo Crime Family Series</u>[2]
<u>Chaos MC series</u>[3]
<u>Savage Ride</u>[4]
Mountain Man Romance:
<u>Men of Blackthorne Mountain Series</u>[5]
<u>Bear's Tooth Mountain Men Series</u>[6]
Cowboy & Small Town Romance:
<u>Roped in by Love Series</u>[7]

---

1. https://books2read.com/u/mqBaze

2. https://books2read.com/u/m0odzW

3. https://books2read.com/u/bMVAOk

4. https://books2read.com/u/bMVlG7

5. https://books2read.com/u/3RYDvB

6. https://books2read.com/u/mVel7A

7. https://books2read.com/u/3RYlBY

About the Author

Hello. I'm Cameron Hart, and I write sweet steamy romances. I'm a *USA Today* Bestselling author with over forty books available. I write romance with lots of heat, plenty of sweet, and just enough drama to keep things interesting. I graduated from the Iowa Writer's Workshop in 2012 with a degree in creative writing. When I'm not working on my next book, I can be found reading, crocheting, doing yoga, and chasing around my grumpy cats.

What to expect from a Cameron Hart book: Lots of heat, plenty of sweet, and just enough drama to keep things interesting. No cheating, safe, guaranteed HEA!

Read more at https://cameronhart.net/.